MVFOL

PENGUIN BOOKS

FRIDA'S BED

Slavenka Drakulić was born in Croatia in 1949. Her nonfiction books include *How We Survived Communism and Even Laughed*, a feminist critique of communism that brought her to the attention of the public in the West; *The Balkan Express: Fragments from the Other Side of the War*, a personal eyewitness account of the war in her homeland; *Café Europa: Life After Communism* (Penguin); and *They Would Never Hurt a Fly* (Penguin). Drakulić is also the author of the novels *Holograms of Fear*, which was a bestseller in Yugoslavia and was short-listed for The Best Foreign Book Award by *The Independent* (UK), *Marble Skin*, *The Taste of a Man* (Penguin), and *S.* (Penguin). A freelance journalist who contributes to *The New York Times*, *The Nation*, *The New Republic*, *Frankfurter Allgemeine Zeitung* (Germany), *Dagens Nyheter* (Sweden), and *La Stampa* (Italy), as well as other magazines and newspapers, she now divides her time among Sweden, Austria, and Croatia.

FRIDA'S BED

A NOVEL

SLAVENKA DRAKULIĆ

TRANSLATED FROM THE CROATIAN BY
CHRISTINA P. ZORIĆ

PENGUIN BOOKS

PENGUIN BOOKS
Published by the Penguin Group
Penguin Group (USA) Inc., 375 Hudson Street, New York, New York 10014, U.S.A.
Penguin Group (Canada), 90 Eglinton Avenue East, Suite 700, Toronto, Ontario,
Canada M4P 2Y3 (a division of Pearson Penguin Canada Inc.)
Penguin Books Ltd, 80 Strand, London WC2R 0RL, England •
Penguin Ireland, 25 St Stephen's Green, Dublin 2, Ireland
(a division of Penguin Books Ltd)
Penguin Group (Australia), 250 Camberwell Road, Camberwell, Victoria 3124, Australia
(a division of Pearson Australia Group Pty Ltd)
Penguin Books India Pvt Ltd, 11 Community Centre, Panchsheel Park,
New Delhi – 110 017, India
Penguin Group (NZ), 67 Apollo Drive, Rosedale, North Shore 0632, New Zealand
(a division of Pearson New Zealand Ltd)
Penguin Books (South Africa) (Pty) Ltd, 24 Sturdee Avenue, Rosebank,
Johannesburg 2196, South Africa

Penguin Books Ltd, Registered Offices:
80 Strand, London WC2R 0RL, England

First published in Penguin Books 2008

1 3 5 7 9 10 8 6 4 2

Copyright © Slavenka Drakulić, 2007
Translation copyright © Christina Pribichevich-Zoric, 2008
All rights reserved

Originally published in Croatian as *Frida ili o boli* by Profil International, Zagreb.

PUBLISHER'S NOTE
This is a work of fiction. Although it draws on events in the life of Frida Kahlo, this work is solely
the product of the author's imagination.

LIBRARY OF CONGRESS CATALOGING IN PUBLICATION DATA
Drakulić Slavenka, 1949–
[Frida, ili, O boli. English]
Frida's bed : a novel / Slavenka Drakulić ; translated by Christina Pribichevich-Zoric.
p. cm.
ISBN 978-0-14-311415-4
1. Kahlo, Frida—Fiction.   I. Pribicevic-Zoric, Christina.   II. Title.
PG1619.14.R34F7513 2008
891.8'336—dc22
2008022382

Printed in the United States of America
Set in Janson
Designed by Ginger Legato

Physical pain does not simply resist language but actively destroys it, bringing about an immediate reversion to a state anterior to language, to sounds and cries a human being makes before language is learned.

—ELAINE SCARRY, *The Body in Pain*

Mi pintura lleva el mensaje del dolor.

—FRIDA KAHLO

FRIDA'S BED

T HAT EARLY JULY MORNING FRIDA WOKE up in her bed at her parents' house. A faint light was already creeping into the room. She had spent a restless night. With an effort, she turned over, propped herself up on the pillows and touched her face as if to make sure that it was still there. She lay there quite still for a while, looking at her arms on the bedcover, then ran her fingers through her hair—her face, her hair, her hands, they were all parts of what had once been a whole. She tried to get out of bed, but then gave up. She had no strength left. Her mind was troubled.

Last year when my leg was amputated it was my—what?—thirty-second operation? Frida tried to remember exactly, touching the scars on her back, her tummy, her leg. I can't remember them all. I wonder if abortions count as operations. Even if I forget those that leave no visible scars I still can't count them all. This counting is useless, she thought.

She looked at the empty spot under the sheet where her sick leg used to be. Strange how she could still feel the half that had been sawed off. That was the same leg, half of the same right leg where the demonic pain had first appeared.

She had been six years old. One morning she woke up with a fever. At first her parents were not worried. Fevers, temperatures, colds, sore throats, diarrhea, vomiting, tummy aches—like all children, their four little girls would occasionally fall ill. They had no reason to suspect that this time it was different.

And then came the pain. First in her leg, as if something had sunk its teeth into it. A huge beast, a dog, maybe. It locked its jaws onto her limb and tore at the muscles with its teeth. She screamed, that was all she could do, scream. She could not describe the feeling of having part of her body ripped apart. She remembered her father's despair, his face as he leaned over her bed, and his words: What is it, tell me, what is it? As she writhed in pain, soaked in her own sweat, Don Guillermo, her kind, good father, waited for her to tell him. For an explanation. A meaningful verbalization of this horror, so that he could understand what was happening to his child. Otherwise, how could he help her? Because her frenzied cries were not enough. Pain needs to be articulated, communicated. It needs a kind of dialogue. It needs words. But only screams and shrieks of pain escaped from the child's lips.

She could still see her leg (her poor little leg, she would say if it didn't sound so pathetic), jerking and twitching on the bed. As if possessed and divorced from the rest of her body. She could see her mother soaking a towel in hot water, the maid's dark hands holding the white porcelain basin, her fingers curled around the rim. She focused on the sparkles in the glistening water, on something that could take her mind off her leg, off herself. To leave her body, that was what she wanted. Or for someone to cut her leg off, because it was not hers anymore. But it kept leaping off the bed as if it had gone mad. She screamed in panic. Her mother wrapped a hot towel around her poor little leg (yes, there it was after all!) and kept saying, she could hear her even now: *Ssh, ssh, it'll go away, it'll go away . . .*

I remember my mother's words because over the years she was to say them again and again. And with reason, except neither of us could know that at the time, a time when this still-unknown, unnamed fiendish beast was tearing away at my flesh, and my mother, wiping the sweat from my forehead, was whispering, *It'll go away.*

And indeed, the pain would ease for a bit, the beast would tire. The child would succumb to the bliss of no pain, only to scream even louder a minute later. The beast had sunk its teeth into her leg and would not let go. As if it had decided to rip it off and devour it.

Her parents finally called in the doctor. The diagnosis: poliomyelitis. The therapy: rest and bed. The consequence: one leg thinner and shorter than the other.

She was bedridden for nine months; an eternity for such a lively child. Since she could not leave her room, she created an imaginary little friend who helped transport her to another world.

Her little friend did not have a name. Frida would blow on the windowpane by her bed and then quickly, quickly trace a door on the foggy glass with her finger. Only the door was very, very small and invisible. The little girl was invisible too, invisible to everybody but her.

Once she had squeezed through the door into this other world, she would find her little friend there waiting for her. Always cheerful and laughing, she would take Frida by the hand and lead her away. Only the two of them inhabited this other world. She could no longer remember her little friend's voice or face; she just knew that they danced in a big empty ballroom, which looked as if it were made of ice. The little girl danced and she followed and talked to her. She talked and talked, and danced. She glided across the floor, twirling and moving with ease. Her crippled leg did not bother her; she did not even feel it. The two of them were a perfect pair. And when she returned to her bed, she felt inexplicably happy for a long time afterward.

In Girl with Death Mask, *a small picture, one of the smallest she ever painted, all you can see on the horizon are the icy snowcapped mountain peaks. A lone girl with a grinning death mask is standing on the hard, dark ground. It is not quite clear whether it is simply a mask or perhaps her own skull. Next to her foot lies another, even more terrifying mask of an animal, its teeth bared, its tongue sticking out, its mouth still red with blood from her leg. The little girl could have worn this mask, but she didn't. It doesn't really matter, though, because the two masks simply represent different forms of death.*

Death has hovered around her since childhood. A shadow that is always there. A ghostly white skull with touches of gray; gray, the color of fear, is ever-present in her life and a part of her.

She is standing there alone beneath the angry sky and swirl of menacing clouds. Still a child, she has yet to grow into her face. When she grows up she will have Frida's face.

Again and again Frida will paint her own face over the white skull, proof that she is still alive.

When she left her bed nine months later, her right leg was withered and ramrod-straight. The other children could not but notice it. They made fun of her at school, calling her Peg-leg. She dreamed of them at night, like foul-snouted coyotes circling ravenously, sniffing menacingly at her leg. She fended them off. She lashed out at them, but she did not cry. At first school was torture for her; later it became a place to practice self-defense.

Knowing how cruel children can be, her mother put extra layers of socks on Frida's right leg to conceal its thinness. But she fooled no one. It was only the new, custom-made pair of boots that gave balance to Frida's walk, if not to her character, which was already showing signs of defiance. The boots made her feel important; she was still only a child, but already she was allowed to wear them like a real young lady. She still kept them in her room, next to her favorite doll, the Aztec figurines the Maestro had given her and the papier-mâché skeleton. The boots were made of fine calfskin, the toes a shade darker than the rest. She remembered how long it took for the maid to lace them up and how she would wait patiently for her to finish. The boots took her back to the days when her father would take her for walks in the countryside. While he painted his watercolors, Frida would collect pretty stones, watch the butterflies, birds and insects.

That was the first time I remember feeling jealous. Not of the other, healthy children, but of all those winged creatures. Once, when a butterfly alighted on my shoulder, flapping its delicate wings, I suddenly burst into tears. I didn't know what to tell my father. I didn't know it was jealousy I was feeling. Why don't I have wings? I asked him. He did not laugh.

Perhaps it had been a sign of the bad times to come, thought Frida as she turned over in her bed that morning.

After recovering from polio, Frida, though still a child, quickly realized that her illness had left its mark. There were two ways she could cope with it: she could give up, accept her lameness as something shameful and hide away in the dark womb of the house—or she could fight back. She was forced at an early age to accept that she was different. But she had yet to learn the most important thing: how to turn her shortcoming into an advantage. That would take years.

When the other children made fun of her, she reacted with anger and defiance, but never self-pity. Young though she was, she refused to accept defeat, that was for Mama's girls, like Kity and her friends. She had always despised tears or any sign of weakness. Since she was different anyway, she might as well be better, faster, stronger. She soon learned how to ride a bike. She climbed trees and swam faster than any of the other little girls who skipped rope and played hopscotch, taking care not to dirty their pretty little dresses. She was better even than Kity, who was not lame, but was not spunky either. And because she was different she could be bold and daring where other little girls could not, she could learn, for instance, how to wrestle or box. Her mother secretly felt sorry for her, but her father was fulsome in his support, telling her that she was better than the others because she was braver, that courage and intelligence were more important than not being lame and that she had both.

Racing around the nearby park on her bicycle, she felt as if she were flying. If only she could fly, she thought, then she would not need legs.

I could not escape the pity or the cruelty of others. Pity had a smell to it, I always recognized it because I had grown up with it. Because it had followed me all my life. Sometimes I thought I would gag from the familiar reek of sweat that soaked the air.

An old auntie, a friend of her grandmother's, would sometimes come calling. She was short and round like a bread roll. She would waddle over to the sofa and sink into the cushions with a sigh, as if these few steps had left her exhausted, and perhaps they had. Then she would take out a fine batiste hankie and wipe her neck and throat. She would bring Frida sweets, the kind that came wrapped in silky paper so they wouldn't stick to your fingers. In return, Frida would let the old lady hug her and stroke her hair with the hand that was not busy gesticulating and dabbing at her sweat, and the old woman would say, Poor, poor little thing! Then, on the verge of tears, she would heave an even louder sigh. She had a peculiar sour-sweet smell to her, a mixture of sweat, vanilla sugar and the mint tea the maid would serve, and also of something indefinable, unusual and strong, like tobacco, but different from the pipe tobacco that Frida's father occasionally smoked. Once she had finished her afternoon tea, she would take out a little silver box, a snuffbox she called it. She would place a pinch of the dark powder on the crook of her finger, raise it to her nose and snort it. Auntie snorted snuff. Don Guillermo, big-boned and tall, would stand by the window and watch her perform this ritual, which little Frida found so fascinating. He did not approve of the child's pretending to like it when the old lady stroked her head just so she could get the sweets, nor did he approve of the old lady's pitying Frida every time she paid a visit. Once, controlling his irritation in front of the child, he could not stop himself from saying, Don't keep telling her what a poor little thing she is, Tante. She looked at him in astonishment, as if the girl's father had taken leave of his senses. But see how she limps, poor little thing, she said sadly. That's just how it looks, said the father, and he walked out of the room, angry, she could tell by his step. Frida took the sweets and hobbled out after him.

In the warm late afternoon air that wafted in through the open garden doors, in the scent of the snuff that mingled with the fragrance of lavender, jasmine and the yellow rambling roses, she recognized the smell of pity. After the old lady left, her father told her that the most important thing was for her not to think of herself as a poor little thing. It had never occurred to her to do so. But she remembered that smell.

The morning light, still faint and diffused, slowly crept in under the dark curtains, circling the furniture and spilling across the floor.

Her nightgown was soaked with sweat, she was shivering, but she took comfort from the fact that, for the moment at least, she was awake and conscious. Because as soon as they gave her the injection, she would drift off into semiconsciousness again. Maybe she could even have a cigarette. But that would require an extra effort. She would have to lift her hand out from under the cover, reach for the cigarettes and matches on the night table, light one up and inhale. And then she would cough until she rued ever having made even the slightest movement. She could hear the birds singing outside. Soon Mayet would wake up and walk into her bedroom with the basin and towel. These morning rituals had become so pointless and tedious. She would rather rest and postpone the start of the day until later.

She tried to recall her life before polio, before her body had become such a burden, before she knew how hard it could be to walk. She remembered hiking in the nearby hills, running after her father and helping him carry his painting kit. Or going to the market with the maid, to mass on Sunday mornings with her mother, to school with Kity . . . Her body was not yet a *hindrance* to her when she walked. But after she recovered from the polio, her body assumed a new weight. Not just physically, she reflected, but metaphysically as well. It became as heavy as a rock that she was forced to drag along. After the accident, there was scarcely a second that she was not conscious of its weight.

She had to admit that there were also times when she knew the meaning of exhilaration and happiness—how else would she have found the strength to drag her body around? And so that morning she tried to recollect the days when it had been such a simple matter to wake up and get out of bed without anybody's help.

If such days had ever existed, they were now lost in the thickening fog that was slowly settling around her like gelatin.

Frida grew up to be an energetic, vivacious girl who wore her hair cropped short and sported trousers. She read poetry, went out with her friends and was in love with Alex. She preferred men to women, her father to her mother, boys to girls. In secondary school there was only one other girl in her crowd of friends, the rest were all boys. A family photograph taken by her father shows her dressed like a man. Her sisters and mother are all wearing elegant dresses, while she is in a man's suit, with vest and tie. Her hair slicked back, holding a cane in her right hand, she looks straight into the camera.

From her expression and demeanor in the photograph, it is difficult to be sure that this is a girl. While her mother and sisters are smiling coquettishly, she remains serious. She even comes across as a bit stiff, arrogant maybe, aware of how provocative her image is in this "official" family photograph. But she could indulge in such behavior because she was her father's favorite. Of his six daughters, she alone received an education. Admittedly, his two daughters from his first marriage were hardly ever mentioned. Doña Matilda had refused to let the girls live with them and so they wound up in a convent. She was not much kinder to her own eldest daughter, who was named after her. When the girl ran away with a boy at the age of fifteen, her mother would not let her return home. The father seemed to have no say in the mother's decisions. He was gentle, introverted, withdrawn. A photographer, after work he would retreat to his room and play the piano or read German philosophy. He never spoke about the life he had left behind or whether he missed Germany, his mother tongue, his studies. His wife Matilda, mother of Matilda, Adriana, Frida and Cristina—or Kity, as they called her—was a decisive woman, pragmatic, obstinate and most of the time ill-tempered. Perhaps it was from her mother that Frida had inherited her tenacity, a certain rigidity, even.

The mother did not think it necessary for Frida to get an education. As with her other three daughters, she taught her everything a woman needed to know in order to get married and have children of her own. She knew how to cook, clean, sew, embroider, knit, so why this unnecessary expense? But the father stood firm. He said Frida was the most like him and since he had not completed his own studies, he was determined that she would finish hers and become a doctor.

Don Guillermo never said he wanted a son, but Frida sensed it and the feeling was confirmed by his smile that day when he photographed the family with her standing in the middle, dressed like a man.

Doña Matilda was illiterate. That had not bothered Frida in the days when she was posing as a man for her father's camera. By the time it did, her mother no longer saw any point in doing anything about it. Learning to read and write? What for? Life is complicated enough as it is, she told her daughter.

Mama was right, Frida mused that morning, how right she was . . .

Later, Frida often thought how strange it was that she had not had even the slightest premonition of the turn her life would take that day. It was September. She was strolling through the marketplace, holding hands with Alex and drinking in the scent of the first autumn rain. The yellow melons and sky-blue dress of a porcelain doll in the antiques shop window caught her eye. She vividly remembered the colors and the piece of orange that Alex had fed her. Its refreshing succulence had made her whole body tingle. The juice trickled down Alex's fingers and she licked them one by one. She and Alex were standing in the street, Alex drowning in her eyes; a breeze caressed her back, she touched the skin under his shirt and a warmth spread through her womb. She knew that passersby were looking at them; a woman smiled.

This moment before the accident, when she was aware of her body from head to toe, was perhaps the last time in her life that she felt whole. Little did she know that only a few seconds later her entire world would be shattered and that nothing would ever be the same again.

Whenever she recalled that day, she would think how her fate had been sealed by the paper parasol Alex had bought her at the market. They were already at the bus stop when she remembered that she had forgotten her parasol somewhere. They ran back and bought another one. It had stopped drizzling just as they were boarding the streetcar. In those days streetcars were still a novelty in town and were made of wood. It was full and they barely managed to find seats together. She would know the faces of the passengers even today, the Indian woman with the turquoise shawl, the man in blue trousers soiled at the knees as if he had been kneeling or had maybe fallen, the woman with a basketful of red chile peppers. The smell of sweat, damp hair and the orange in Alex's hand. She could feel the touch of his leg through her skirt.

The streetcar was about to turn a corner when there was a screech of the brakes. Then a crash and the sound of wood splintering and glass shattering. Frida felt neither the blow nor pain.

It is not true that you feel something when you are in an accident. There is no feeling, no thought. You do and you do not exist, like a particle of dust swirling in the air. You see the blue sky and you are a part of it, you are a part of the air, the water, the greenery in the park. You drift in a silence where you cannot even hear the beating of your own heart. Isn't that the experience of nothingness?

And quiet, yes, she remembered the quiet. That was really

her only memory of the accident. When she was a child she
would fold a sheet of paper over several times and then with
a pair of scissors cut out symmetrical shapes. Her paper sun
had sun rays, but it lacked a center. Her memory of the accident was like that sun with a hole in the middle.

She did not know how long she was absent from her body.
The next thing she remembered was the woman with the
peppers running and holding her own guts in her hands. She
heard someone calling for help and then someone else shouting, "Ballerina, ballerina." How silly, she thought, what is he
talking about? She lifted her arm and saw that it was covered
in blood and dusted with gold. The scene was unreal, as if she
had suddenly been transported to the theater. Or was already
dead.

I remembered that red is both the color of life and the
color of death. Later, whenever I tried to remember my
crushed body, the blood and the gold dust, I would think
how mine was a life of color and kitsch even then. Had I ever
painted the accident itself I would have used those two colors.
But that is the one picture I never painted, however much it
underlaid all my work.

Because all I ever really painted was my accident, she
thought as she gazed out the window that morning.

Later, she learned that the crash had left her lying naked in
the street, her blood-streaked body dusted with gold powder
which a house painter had probably been carrying. She remembered a man leaning over her, pressing his knee against
her stomach and yanking out something lodged deep inside

her. Suddenly blood gushed out and spilled down her thighs. She screamed and lost consciousness again.

She came to in the hospital. Alex, who had walked away from the accident miraculously unhurt, later told her that her right leg, the lame one, had been broken in eleven places and her right foot had been dislocated and crushed. Her lower spine was broken in three places, her collarbone was broken and so were two ribs. Her left shoulder was dislocated. The doctors would be able to patch everything back together again except for the spine and fractured pelvis, he said. Then he described what he had seen with his own eyes: a long metal rod—the handrail—had ripped into her stomach near her left hip and come out through her vagina.

She had been impaled alive. At the hospital, people rushed her through the corridors on a stretcher, shouting, Hurry, hurry, hurry. In the operating room the white-masked nurse leaned over her and said, Take a deep breath and count to ten. She inhaled the ether, never dreaming how many more times in her life she would be subjected to its smell. Finally she drifted off into blissful oblivion.

The doctors were not sure if she would survive. But survive she did. Her young body fought back. She recovered, immediately learning how to accustom herself to the pain that had taken up residence in her body and become a subtenant she would never be able to evict.

The man who had had the presence of mind to pull the rod out of her body helped Alex lay Frida out on the billiard table in a nearby bar while they waited for help. You lay there on the green felt, naked, covered in blood and dusted in gold.

Passersby thought you were an injured bar dancer, that's why they called you ballerina. You were so beautiful, Alex told her the day after the operation as he sat by her side, holding her hand.

When she was a child she had had to learn how to lie still, and this proved useful after the operation. Immobile, encased in a cast from head to foot, for the first few days all she could do was cry. I'm used to pain so that's good, she told Alex, as if he, not she, needed comforting. She survived and, despite the pain, felt relieved. But from time to time she would be overwhelmed by an entirely new awareness of how fragile and transparent everything around her was. Having seen death from the other side, she had come to an icy certainty. As if she had suddenly acquired the ability to see through people and past her own reality.

In the hospital that old feeling of her body being a foreign entity returned—that experience of self-separation she remembered when she had escaped to the little girl on the other side of the windowpane. She became aware of her body as a mechanism; the heightened sharpening of all her senses allowed her to keep track of the pain—when it appeared and where, how each part of this mechanism functioned quite irrespective of her conscious will, like an automaton. She realized how much the condition of her body affected her feelings, behavior, thoughts. The fact that this was *her body* no longer meant the same thing to her after the accident.

She had already learned (polio: lesson number one) how difficult it is to imagine somebody else's pain, even when that somebody else is one's own child. Her mother was struck dumb with shock and her father fell ill. His health had already deteriorated from the increasingly frequent epileptic seizures that plagued him. During the month that she was immobilized in the hospital her mother visited her twice and her father only once. It all seemed too much for them. Had it not been for her sister Matilda, Alex and her school friends, she would have been utterly alone. She shared a room with twenty other patients, lying on her back in a coffinlike plaster carapace. She could not move a single part of her body except for the toes of her left foot and the fingers of her left hand.

At first the pain was unbearable. Again she lacked the words to explain how excruciating it was. She could say that it was a piercing pain and that it penetrated every part of her body. But she gave up before even starting. Not only would no one understand, but soon they would get tired of trying. How could she describe a body on fire, a searing wound? By using these words? She knew that words would not help people feel what she felt. Once when she was at church with her mother and sisters, a young woman collapsed in the middle of the priest's sermon. Her limbs started shaking uncontrollably and a terrifyingly deep, menacing male voice issued from her mouth. It's the devil, the devil, cried the priest, frantically brandishing the cross over her.

I am possessed, she thought with horror as she lay there in the hospital, convinced that that same demon was now inhabiting her flesh and bones.

She thought it would be easier to bear the pain if someone

at least knew how she felt. She consoled herself the only way she knew how, the way her mother had taught her. It'll go away, she would tell her visitors. When I recover everything will be the same as it was before. Alex agreed. Of course it will, he told her, of course everything will be the same.

At night she watched death flit around her bed and dreamed of being a yellow butterfly.

Later, much later, she painted a picture that she called The Dream. *It took time and strength for her to paint it. The first few nights in the hospital she was afraid that death would claim her in her sleep. How to defeat death? How to cheat death? How to drive it away? She felt better once she had drawn the skeleton. Like the papier-mâché skeletons they sold at the market on the Day of the Dead, her own painted death became something of a household fixture. She laid the skeleton down on her bed and propped the skull up with two pillows to make it more comfortable. She placed a bouquet of flowers in its hands.*

Thus she gave shape to her fear, but this did not mollify death. What is disturbing in the painting is not the skeleton, but the plant above the sleeping Frida, spreading its roots, weaving its web, waiting.

She spent another three months bedridden at home. A wall rose around her. She was already isolated, her hopes shattered, trapped in a body that would never recover and from which she could escape only occasionally.

But her crushed body did not stop her from being loud and demanding. Once again she heard her mother's voice saying, *It'll go away*, like a magic incantation that would restore her health. She did not know how else to comfort her daughter. Doña Matilda did not understand why such a tragedy had to befall her family. As a good Catholic, she agonized over this question and looked to heaven for an answer. Why did the good Lord, to whom she prayed every day, let her daughter suffer so much? Wasn't it enough that she had had polio and that it had marked her for life? Or was God punishing her, Matilda? Frida knew that early every morning, before the insufferable heat set in, her mother would go to the nearby church, dip her fingers in the holy water of the stone font at the entrance, kneel and cross herself. Then she would sit down in a back pew, pull her scarf down over her brow like an old woman and pray, pray for God to take pity on her poor unfortunate child.

Her nerves already frayed, Doña Matilda tortured herself with further doubts. Frida, not wishing to add to her mother's worries, pretended to be brave. And brave she was, with a touch of pathos in her lies, trying to dispel any concerns those closest to her might have. Look at me, why, I'm fine, getting better and better, she would say. Don't worry about me, Mama, I'll survive. She found the strength to cheer up others and cut short the pity she so despised. After a few months, when Frida really was better, Doña Matilda commissioned a thanksgiving mass, convinced her prayers had been heard. For a while—quite a while, in fact—her humor improved.

Frida never asked herself why this had had to happen to her. She did not believe there was anyone who had the answer to such a question.

Once she was better and the pain in her back and leg became bearable, boredom set in. She asked her friends to visit, to write and send her books. She had the cook prepare special dishes, made only for her. She asked Kity to stay and keep her company, the way she used to. In her letters to Alex, she complained about how bored she was and how she envied him his coming travels around Europe. But boredom was a sign that she was on the mend.

Sometimes she would embroider linen, but mostly she read. Doña Matilda knew, however, that her daughter could not spend all her time reading. She thought painting might be the answer. Frida had spent that summer working at the printing shop of a friend of her father's. She would come home talking excitedly about the Swedish artist Anders Zorn, whose paintings she copied. Her father had taught her how to retouch photographs and she was already well versed in color tones and brushstrokes. He would sometimes commend her patience and concentration. And so Doña Matilda decided that painting might provide Frida with a temporary distraction and pastime until she fully recovered. Once her bones had set and she could stand up, she would have no need of it anymore. That was what she told her daughter the morning when she brought her the paints and brushes, brushes Frida knew well because they were her father's.

Her mother, she recalled, stood by her bed wearing a dark brown satin dress that accentuated her pale complexion. She had not been feeling well for quite some time; she would be beset by acute stomach pains, which would eventually disappear only to reoccur a month or two later. She was also plagued by headaches that would often make her take to her bed for the whole day. They were not close, the two of them; indeed, Doña Matilda was not close to any of her four daughters, with the possible exception of Kity, who was still like a child and never contradicted her mother. There was a void between mother and daughters, a distance that was filled by servants who cooked and washed and took care of them, women whose large languid bodies stood between the girls and their mother. There was too little physical contact, there were too few hugs and embraces. She always felt that her mother was present, but it was as if she were in another room, never completely there, moody, sad and unwell herself.

So she was surprised when her mother brought her the paints and brushes. Frida had never thought of painting. Here, this may catch your fancy, her mother said, painting will help you relax and take your mind off the accident. Frida noticed that it was hard for Doña Matilda to utter the word. Her mother showed her the small lap-easel she had had made so that it could be placed on the bed. She felt a lump rise in her throat and tears sting her eyes. She was grateful to her mother for showing how worried she was about her health.

Her mother did not usually demonstrate love so openly and she was certain that at that moment Doña Matilda believed her daughter would never walk again.

She clasped her mother's hand and kissed it. Doña Matilda found herself flustered. She stroked her daughter's brow, turning her head away to hide her emotions. She could not bear to watch her vivacious child lying there so immobile, so hurt and battered and yet so patient. She told herself that everything would be better once Frida was no longer bedridden and they finally removed the cast. She would forget all her pain, her scars would heal and life would pick up where it had left off.

She had been playing various sports, even soccer, since the age of six, and so she was as strong, muscular and quick as a boy. After the accident, when she was bedridden and not allowed to move, she had to unlearn everything she had been taught. She practiced immobility. She practiced endurance. First there was the excruciating pain. Then she was driven mad by having to lie still. Her little childhood friend was not there anymore to help her. But she remembered what her little friend had taught her (lesson number two!): when the pain rivets you to your body you have to step out of yourself if you are to survive. Once again she had to find a way to lie still and at the same time be somewhere else—and someone else. Her mother's suggestion about painting intrigued her. And when her father came up with the idea of fixing a mirror above her bed so that she could see her own face, she began to paint what was closest at hand—herself.

Ever since the accident, her father had not been himself. He had become more withdrawn than ever; he barely opened his mouth now. Her mother would serve him dinner herself. He would eat alone, not uttering a word, and then shut himself away in his room and play the piano. Don Guillermo came from Europe, from another world and another time, and he never seemed to have completely joined them in theirs. She found his sadness hard to bear. Especially as he had no God to turn to. Sometimes she wondered how her mother could live with such an incredibly introverted, sad man.

At the time I knew too little about men, about living as a couple, about whether it is better for them to be quiet or chatty, she thought, wide awake now. Her room was still cloaked in darkness. But it was no longer the nocturnal, velvety, cozy darkness of the womb. The light seemed to have a life, a mission of its own: to subject her to yet another day.

She was convinced that the demonic pain she had suffered in her leg as a child had been in some sort of preparation for the accident. Engraved in her memory was how she had been left speechless by the first attack. She had yet to accept that pain cannot be expressed in words but only in inarticulate screams. It took time before she could put brush to canvas, and still more time before she could paint pictures that screamed. In place of the screams themselves. In place of verbal descriptions. She owed it to her father, she thought, to the frantic look in his eyes which she would never forget, and to his words: *Tell me, tell me!*

The first time she picked up the paintbrush to paint she was lying in the same room she had been in as a child with polio, only this time she was condemned to a lifetime of pain. It was no longer just one illness now. The pain had distributed itself throughout her body, taking up its positions in preparation to stay.

Such a long period of immobility had heightened her powers of observation. Nothing seemed simple or small anymore; it was like seeing the world through a magnifying glass.

She distinguished almost invisible markings on the seemingly smooth surfaces of the objects in her room. She noticed details she had never paid attention to before: the interweaving thin and thick threads that unevenly coursed the bed linen; the little cracks and crevices collecting dust on the once smooth and white wall; she was bothered by the irregularities in the embroidered roses on her pillow—when, in a moment of inattention, someone's hand (her mother's? her sister's?) had threaded the red just a millimeter off the traced blue line, a moment when someone had perhaps entered the room and called her name, disturbing her concentration. There was a light diagonal streak down the dark brown leg of the little table, as if a cat had scratched it. But why would a cat scratch the table leg? she wondered. And that thought transported her into another world, imagining hands, imagining cats.

In her suddenly diminished world, which she felt was getting smaller by the day, she saw faces in a new light as well. She paid more attention to facial features, expressions, grimaces, the different tones of voice and colors of clothes. As if being bedridden somehow made her notice things more and gradually lent the world new, intriguing dimensions.

She saw even herself differently. Looking at her face in the mirror, she noticed that her youthful skin didn't match her dark, almost scowling gaze. I am getting old, she thought, age is already showing in my eyes. I feel as if I learned everything all at once, in an instant. My friends are gradually becoming women, but I aged instantaneously. It is as if everything has become quite simple and I know that there is nothing there on the other side, because if there were, I would see it, she wrote to Alex.

She was now painting almost every day—sketches, studies and portraits of the people around her, but mostly of herself. This was no longer merely a pastime. Painting completely absorbed her. She assiduously studied the history of European art, especially the work of the great Renaissance masters, and she practiced the steadiness of her hand. She progressed quickly, her hand becoming ever surer, achieving what she wanted ever quicker. She was pleased with the self-portrait she painted for Alex. She sent it to him, out of despair, out of love, out of the need to feel him nearer. She spent words and words on him, she wrote to him every day, but it was not enough. And he wrote to her, but his letters were polite somehow, already distant and cold. As if he had given them to an adult to read before mailing them. Alex was her first love and she could not accept the idea that her accident could drive them apart. Her wretched condition was only temporary; just be patient, Alex, she wrote to him at the beginning. But Alex was drifting away and while she was still recovering he was getting ready to travel.

Alex had been the leader of their little group. He had made school less of a bore. They had been together for three years, from the beginning of secondary school until the accident. It was probably he who had saved her life. His visits to her in the hospital became fewer and farther between, and then he left. In order to separate him from his bedridden girlfriend, his parents, to whom it was clear that the accident had left her permanently disabled, sent him on a long voyage to Europe. As far away from her as possible. Later she wondered whether Alex had sensed even then how much the accident would change their relationship.

In Self-Portrait, *the expression on her face is soft, the look melancholic, with a trace of a sad smile. Her body presents a hidden challenge, but her face is serious, the eyes quiet and sorrowful. The painting suggests gentleness, tenderness, spirituality. And loneliness in the enveloping blackness that separates her from her environment. This is Frida's only self-portrait where she is still a gentle, vulnerable, strikingly feminine girl who seems to be asking Alex to protect her. This softness is absent from her later self-portraits, where it is as if she had donned a suit of armor. Or a mask.*

That same year she painted a portrait of her sister Adriana, wearing a dress with a plunging neckline. Her shoulders and breasts seem to be spilling out of the dress, which looks as if it is about to slip off the smooth white skin and bare her voluptuous body. It is as if Frida had deliberately painted this portrait as the exact opposite of herself. There is not a trace of restraint or refinement in Adriana, she is pure sensuality. However, there is a light in the cloudy sky behind her, a cupola with an illuminated window. For her there is hope, whereas for Frida there is only dark, enclosed space.

It was only much later that she realized how different this painting was from all her other self-portraits. And it was not just because of her artistic inexperience. This first self-portrait was different because she had painted it with a secret motive—she wanted it to win back Alex for her. It was a clear attempt to lure Alex back the only way left open to her.

After receiving her portrait, Alex did return to her and for a while they were together again. Frida was already becoming aware of what would later become the hallmark of her paintings: their power of speech.

Suddenly she grew up. As if until the accident she had been living without any real awareness of herself, like a baby monkey leaping from branch to branch, screeching in delight, with occasional reminders that it was not quite like the others. She remembered that feeling, that periodic bliss of self-oblivion, though ever since childhood she had sensed the hovering presence of a dark shadow overhead. Sometimes, lying on her back in the yard, gazing up at the square patch of sky framed by the walls of the houses, out of nowhere a cloud would appear in the clear blue sky, suddenly darkening the yard. And she would shiver. Or she would crawl into bed at night exhausted and just before dropping off, her eyes already closed, her body curled up under the scratchy sheet (she could still feel it even now, in that same bed), she would sometimes imagine the touch of a cold hand. Such unexpected moments left her shuddering.

Yet, her growing power of resistance made her quickly forget it all. The euphoria that usually followed reminded her of playing hide-and-seek or a game of chess. As if she had escaped death one moment only to be dealt an even harder blow the next.

I know now that everything after the accident was merely a tactic to indulge in escapism and self-delusion. When you are hit by a streetcar that almost smashes you to a pulp, when you experience your own end . . . there is no recovery, only temporary respite, she thought.

Pain made me aware of my body. My body made me aware of deterioration and death. That awareness made me old. My death sentence may have been deferred, but I now had to live with a twofold realization. Not only was I going to die—there was nothing unusual about that except that I was made to realize it at a tender age—but I knew exactly what that meant. Because I had already been through it. Unlike other condemned people for whom death is an abstraction because they have no idea what really awaits them, my stay of death came with a constant reminder, the presence of pain.

She was nineteen before she finally stood on her feet again. The money for her education had run out. She had to find a job. The only thing she had learned to do during her convalescence was paint. At a party she met the Maestro, Mexico's most famous painter, and afterward she got it into her head that she had to show him her paintings. He would tell her, she decided, whether there was any point to her plan. It never occurred to her that the Maestro might refuse. She had been unusually willful even as a child, but after the accident she became positively bullish. She dared to do what others didn't because she had the courage of someone who has nothing to lose.

She set off for the building where the Maestro was working on a fresco. Since she could not carry her canvases up to the scaffold, she asked him to come down. Intrigued by the petite girl with the husky voice, the Maestro climbed down.

He walked over to Frida and studied her interesting face, with its full mouth and thick black eyebrows. Without flinching, she looked him straight in the eye. She had brought three of her paintings with her. They were leaning against the front wall of the building he was working on. She turned the pictures around for him to see. She had no time to lose, she said, she was in urgent need of work. She painted because she found it the easiest and least boring of occupations. It would be good if she could earn some money from it. The Maestro's opinion of her work would determine if she should be looking for another occupation, since she had no intention of deluding herself that she was talented if she wasn't. Could he help her by telling her the truth? She said it all in a rush, without pausing for breath. Then she folded her arms across her chest and looked at him.

She did not tell him that painting had been her only salvation from the isolation in which she had been living, that she liked how painting completely absorbed her and that when she painted she felt as if she had rediscovered her little friend in the ice palace.

The Maestro looked at the paintings carefully; her request was unusual, but he liked her explanation, especially when she said that she found painting the least boring way to earn money. He was touched by her decisiveness and seriousness. She stood there waiting, impatient, tense. The Maestro was taking too long to examine the paintings.

She was unquestionably talented, he told her, but he wanted to see more of her work before pronouncing upon something so important. She invited him to visit her at her parents' house. He promised he would. Only then did she breathe a sigh of relief. If the Maestro liked her other canvases as well, perhaps she really could earn a living from painting. All she could think about at the time was money, and her father who no longer had enough work. He had become more and more depressed. The days when Don Guillermo could earn a decent living as a photographer were long gone. And then there was her mother, worn out by her daughter's illness and her own, by obligations and the fear of poverty. Frida had survived the accident but her doctors, medicine and leg braces still had to be paid for. If the Maestro gave her his support, maybe things would change.

A few days later, when he saw her small home exhibition, the Maestro was no longer in any doubt that he had before him an exceptional talent. You must paint, he told her seriously. He was looking at her and her paintings as if he could not get enough of them. It was as if he could not entirely separate the paintings from the unusual person who had done them. What especially impressed the Maestro was the fact that she had preferred to paint rather than use her illness as an excuse to do nothing. There was something unusual, admirable about this girl, about her brusqueness, her thirst for life that was so evident in her every movement. Moreover, he discovered that she had recently joined the Communist Party, which gave them something else in common. After art, politics was the second most important thing in his life, but for her and her new artist friends, like Tina Modotti, ideology was less important than the opportunity it gave them to be together.

Her hair was splayed out on the pillow, damp and sticky to the touch. The odd streak of gray flecked her still-thick dark mane. It occurred to her that she ought to wash it, but then she laughed at her own automatic reaction. Her body would not respond just like that. She lifted her hand and brushed away the stray wisps from her brow. Her hair was the only part of her that was still alive. Her father had had a luxuriant head of hair. She remembered how he would sometimes stop in midsentence and run his fingers through it and how she had loved that gesture, that sign of absentmindedness. He would tell her that her hair was as strong as a horse's. The Maestro would bury his head in it, inhaling its fragrance. He would tell her something quite different, that her hair was as soft as the finest silk. She always thought of him when she brushed her hair, how he would unbraid it at night and she would feel his warm breath on her neck. And how these two most important men in her life saw her hair so differently.

She was alone in the room. Her father had died long ago and the Maestro was in another woman's bed. Kity was tired and her friends were far away. She was increasingly afraid of the light and the inexorable advent of day.

As day broke, she thought of that first meeting with the Maestro and what she would tell him if he were here with her now.

Maestro, she would say, I remember the first time I undressed and stood naked in front of you. I hesitated, of course. I was so young, twenty years younger than you, and so unsure of myself—my only weapon was to be bold. I decided to test you by showing you my body, starting with my back.

I wish I could have seen your eyes as they examined me. My withered leg. The scars from my operations, all the things that were for my doctor's eyes only. I wanted you, but at the same time I was afraid, my heart was in my mouth. Climbing the stairs up to your studio, I said to myself, No, I won't undress in front of him, I can't risk losing him so soon, I care about him too much. And the next moment I decided to do the exact opposite. I will undress, immediately, let him look, let him see everything right away! I won't play hide-and-seek, not with this man. If my body disgusts him, I'll survive. I've survived worse. I'm armor-protected both inside and out, I've got thick skin.

But all the while I hoped you would recognize that other me, the one not visible to the naked eye, the one who lives deep in a hole and comes out only in the paintings.

And then we entered your studio. All I remember is the light, bright, sharp, unrelenting. As soon as you closed the door you grabbed me in your arms in that way that later became familiar. I pushed you away, hard. You lost your balance for a moment, surprised by my roughness, and I laughed. You thought it was a game, that I was playacting, and then in the middle of your studio I stripped naked and turned my back to you. Go ahead, take a good look, I said. First look at my back and all the scars from all the operations, and at my withered leg and crooked foot, and then come here if you've got the guts, if you still want me.

Had I ever thought of myself as a cripple before then? I loathed the very word. Why would anyone be useless just because she was lame? I rejected the very idea that the word could apply to me, even though I had known since childhood that that was what people thought when they saw me limping. When we first met, I felt good and only occasionally did I drag my leg. When I showed you my body in the clear light of day in your studio, I understood for the first time the true meaning of the word because it was inscribed down the length of my back by the crude incisions of the surgeon's scalpel. I was marked. Branded. I felt humiliated and afraid, the way I used to when I was a child riding my bike through the park and the other little girls would call out after me, There goes Peg-leg! Maestro, I could not even imagine what a painter who had possessed the most beautiful women in the world would see in me. I felt your probing eyes move down my back, stopping at each scar as if to inspect my map of pain. I don't know how long I stood there like that. When I turned around you looked at me, wide-eyed, as if I were a ghost.

Then you picked me up in your arms. You laid me down in the copper tub and turned on the water. I lay there, my eyes closed, while you soaped me down, your hand carefully touching my skin as if you were afraid of hurting me. For the first time I felt sure that I was not alone anymore. And then a miracle occurred, Maestro, you recognized me, and that is why I want you with me now, I do and I do not want you.

No one has ever been as naked as I was then. Normal people are merely naked. But my body was both naked and wounded—it was vulnerable. My scars did not frighten you. It is through scars that one touches a person's solitude. I learned that from you, with you, that day.

Later I painted those scars, to let others reach into my solitude.

She looked again at the bedcover, for the leg that was no longer there, though it still felt like a living part of her. She could even wiggle her toes.

When she thought of all the humiliation she had suffered because of that leg! It struck her that this was the same leg that the Maestro's ex-wife Lupe had made fun of at her wedding twenty-five years earlier. It was not until they had finally amputated the leg she had so reluctantly dragged around all of her life that she realized the woman had been right . . . The beautiful Lupe had been drunk and miserable because the Maestro was marrying Frida. It was nightfall by the time they had gathered in the sitting room (cognac, tequila), people were dancing, drinking, sitting on the divan. And then, at one moment, Lupe flipped open the slit in her narrow black skirt and displayed her long white bare leg. "Maestro, look at what you're missing," she said loudly, too loudly. Lupe knew what she was doing, she knew that there could never be any comparison between her and his new wife, not in that sense. Even Frida's good leg was no match for hers. Lupe stood there motionless (or did it just seem that way?), like a magnificent marble sculpture, her whiteness dazzling in the semidark room.

Everyone saw her performance, they could hardly have missed it. The smoke, the music, the sound of laughter. Lupe in her elegant, clinging evening gown, her shoulders bare. And Frida in her peasant costume, borrowed from the maid to please the Maestro. To her mother's horror, she had discarded the white wedding gown on the bed. Furious now, Frida felt like gouging the eyes out of this stupid woman who was humiliating her at her own wedding.

Doña Matilda, who was dressed more for a funeral than for a wedding, also saw the proffered leg. Stern and stiff, she was the exact opposite of Lupe, but also of her own daughter, who was more like Lupe than either one of them would have liked. Frida looked at her mother and noticed that she was blinking rapidly, as if she could not see properly or could not believe her own eyes. She knew her mother's body language only too well, her reservedness, her fear of closeness, of physical contact. The lapse lasted only a second. Then Doña Matilda pulled herself together, reverted to form and quickly turned away. For something like that to happen at her daughter's wedding, for his ex-wife to bare herself publicly like that! Was there no end to the shame her daughters would bring down upon her? Matilda had run away from home . . . And this one had married an old man, wearing the maid's clothes, yet! And now this scandal with the leg.

Doña Matilda flinched, as if she had been scalded, as if she had never seen a bare leg before. Frida saw how horrified her mother was, not so much by the sight of a firm, smooth body as by the thought of what it might arouse in a man. She was hurt by her mother's obvious, perpetual fear of another woman. Even at the wedding Doña Matilda did not believe that her poor infirm daughter could emerge victorious. And if she did, the victory would be short-lived. She would not be able to parry the beautiful women who constantly surrounded the painter—rumors about him had reached even her ears. Doña Matilda already sensed how hard the fight to hold on to the Maestro would be, and how much Frida would suffer.

But the leg so provocatively displayed was a slap in Frida's face as well. Lupe's behavior shocked her, and for the first time since meeting the Maestro she had doubts about whether she would be able to hold her own with all these women hovering around him. She was grateful to the Maestro for having chosen her over Lupe. She was still too young to understand that the scene that had just taken place had been for her benefit, not the Maestro's. She could not yet know what she was about to find out, that his latest wedding was not the beginning of a new chapter in his life. The Maestro would continue to chase pretty girls, because in his mind they had nothing to do with his love for Frida, his third wife.

The Maestro had already had quite a bit to drink. When Doña Matilda turned her back on the scene, Frida did not notice the look on his face. In the dusk of the smoke-filled room and the subdued lamplight, he could not but see Lupe's alabaster white leg. He could not but hear her taunting comment, but he decided to ignore her and simply turned around to resume his conversation. What she saw was a man, her husband, for whom the entire performance had been amusing. She breathed a sigh of relief. A sense of superiority filled her. She walked over to the drunken Lupe and held her up so that she would not fall. I've got a headache, said Lupe, collapsing, her eyes closed and quite faint now. Somebody brought her a glass of water. Frida dipped a napkin in the water and placed it on Lupe's brow. Frida had before her a beautiful woman who was losing the battle to a cripple. I'm sorry, Lupe mumbled, not looking at her. There is nothing to be sorry about, Frida said, savoring her own generosity. It was not until later, when she remembered Lupe's words and realized that she herself was the loser, that she understood the full cruelty of the situation.

But at that moment, on her wedding day, she thought how, even though she did not have the voluptuous body of a Lupe, it was her the Maestro had chosen, her whom he loved. It was a moment of triumph for her youth and her self-confidence. And her mother, who worried about Frida from a distance, never let her know what she was about to find out for herself: that her victory would be short-lived; that victory and defeat are brother and sister; that a beautiful leg will always win out over a lame one, that is simply how things are. And that love can—exceptionally—grow into something quite different, into something that has nothing to do with what kind of legs you have. But Frida did not understand that yet and could not bear this cursed fear of rejection that afflicts women. It was a feeling she would soon know herself.

She never forgot the incident or the three women of such disparate experience—the beautiful abandoned Lupe, the naïve sick Frida and the shocked Catholic mother. And in the background were the men, the Maestro, her father, her friends, all of them behaving as if such hysterical female outbursts had nothing to do with them. The scene was drowned out by the music and loud buzz of conversation.

But whenever she thought of it, she was always hurt by

the recollection of her mother gathering up the folds of her dress, turning on her heel and walking out of the room, her shoulders slightly stooped, looking defeated somehow.

Soon after the wedding, she realized that the Maestro's love for her was not to the exclusion of other women.

Of course he's got an eye for other women, she would say to herself; take a better look at yourself, open your eyes. Darling Maestro, my illness, or, let's be precise about it, my illnesses, were your best ally. I was grateful that you even deigned to notice me. I was so plain and awkward, and cheeky, to boot. I was a nobody, a talented beginner who splashed paint on canvas and dreamed about supporting her family by selling her artwork. And you were famous, the most famous painter and ladies' man in all of Mexico. I knew that, of course, everybody knew it, but like my two predecessors I thought that I, with my limitless love, would somehow manage to change and domesticate you. Because, of course, no one had ever loved you as much as I did.

But then for the first time I realized that— No, no, that's not how it was, I hadn't understood a thing. I had been too infantile, too self-confident. You told me about it yourself, in passing, you mentioned your latest "assistant," Iona. Oh, yes, I remember the moment, her name, that feeling of numbness when I can still see, still hear, but am not there anymore: I can't feel my arms or my legs, my heart has stopped beating; I cannot move, I cannot utter a single word; I am floundering; I am disappearing . . . You hold me up and stop me from collapsing; you sit me down on a chair;

you look worried, but I see it all from a distance; I feel removed, numb.

I must admit I was both stunned and fascinated by the incidental way in which you mentioned that you were sleeping
with another woman. It was in a conversation, not in a fight
or an argument, but in an ordinary conversation. Because for
you sex with other women—with your "models," your "as-
sistants," your lady friends and protégés—was exactly that,
incidental. They were always around, close at hand. They
surrounded you like air. At first I tried to understand your
need to conquer, to possess beautiful women as being part of
your artistic nature, part of your striving for absolute beauty
in everything. But it turned out that painting simply gave you
opportunities other men didn't have. The women were often
naked—you liked to paint nudes and this was a way to possess them—and they were laid out to your eye, your touch
and all your senses. Like on a platter. You painted them, but
you reacted like the male of the species. Your behavior left no
room for thought, it never occurred to you that your actions
could hurt me. That day, when I first realized the nature of
your relationship with Iona, you tried to tell me how such
things weren't important to you. You said that it was just a
superficial, physical relationship. *Physical*, you said, that is the
word you used. How could you have been so thoughtless to
say that to me—me, whose body has terrorized my entire life?
But I was so taken aback that I said nothing.

There is a photograph of you, Maestro, standing with
María Félix in front of your portrait of her. She is standing in
profile, wearing a light-colored dress. Bare-shouldered, her

dark thick hair tumbling down her back. You are standing next to each other, your bodies almost (but not yet) touching. Her right hand is on your shoulder. It is almost possessive. She is looking you straight in the eye as if to say, You're mine! You are already a gentleman of a certain age, with thinning hair and a slight stoop. You are looking at her with such a blissful smile on your face that the photograph remains etched in my memory. At first I thought you were admiring her beauty and that that was why you were reveling in her presence. It was pure chance that it was María Félix and not some other stunner, I told myself when I saw the photograph in the papers. And I would not have been upset, I wouldn't have thought twice about it, had you not been holding her by the elbow. The two of you looked as if you had been caught dancing and were about to twirl out of sight. It was how you were holding her that gave you away. It was too intimate. I realized, Maestro, that you knew this dazzling, raven-haired woman only too well. The pain of it was like a migraine that suddenly takes hold of you, lasts for days and never quite goes away. You live in a state of anticipation, a fear of when it will strike next.

In those first years of her marriage Frida only dabbled in painting. She was untrue to herself, ignoring her talent, the very thing that had so captivated the Maestro. He became more important to her than painting. She thought he had found a way into her inner self, buried deep inside her prison. Occasionally she would put brush to canvas and paint, portraits mostly, nothing dramatic, nothing painful or bloody yet. There was money, she no longer had to worry about that.

She needed to find the strength to go on painting next to one of the world's greatest painters. She was surrounded by his fame and at first it made her feel even more unsure of herself. The papers wrote about her as his charming wife, not as a painter. The talented young woman who had no training, did not sell or exhibit her pictures, became aware of her status as the Maestro's wife as soon as they married. She almost completely lost her self-confidence.

So her new goal was at least to become a good wife, to learn how to cook the Maestro's favorite dishes, which she would bring him in a flower-festooned basket to his scaffold. She even changed the way she looked. For him dress was a class issue, a part of the popular national ideology of "Mexicanism." She wanted to hold his attention and keep him fascinated. She knew that he liked the peasant costumes of the Mexican women of Tehuana. Suddenly she began wearing long skirts and colorful shawls, with flowers and ribbons in her hair; people turned in amazement when they saw her in the street. Yesterday's city girl deliberately transformed herself from a modern young woman who liked wearing trousers, leather jackets and men's boots into a Tehuana peasant woman. Initially, the exotic clothes were her way of playing up to him; only later did it become a part of her individualism and style. Everyone who knew her found her transformation astonishing. But it was for the Maestro that she dressed, that she cooked, that she lived.

Ideology was yet another way for her to be close to the

Maestro. Surrounded by poverty and sensitive to injustice, she shared his belief in the ideology of communism and the idea of justice. And for her the Maestro, who in her universe stood head and shoulders above everybody else, increasingly personified communism.

Two years after their wedding, she painted their portrait, Frida and Diego Rivera. *Wearing a wide dark green skirt and red shawl, she is standing next to the Maestro, holding his hand. Her head is coquettishly tilted toward him, as if she is about to rest it on his shoulder any minute. The Maestro is holding a palette and brushes in his right hand. He is an artist. Her hands are empty. She is simply the artist's wife; she looks like an ordinary Mexican peasant woman. This painting has none of the seductive quality of her first self-portrait or the seriousness of her later work. She painted herself, but it is as if this is not her. Sweet and submissive, there is no stamp of personality here. No trace of the intriguing girl, the painter, the fascinating woman-to-be that the Maestro had fallen in love with. He is in the center of the painting; she is a mere appendage, a reflection, a shadow.*

Having transformed and reinvented herself, her primary public role was as the exotic wife of a great artist. It was this, more than her paintings, that captivated the public. Now every morning she would dress as if about to go on stage. She displayed the professionalism of someone who steps back before choosing the best costume for her role that day. Every detail reflected how she perceived that role. There was nothing spontaneous about her appearance, it was all about self-representation. Her choice of clothes allowed her to step into her role and perform.

She had mastered the technique of dissociation, of separating from her body, long ago when as a child she would escape through an imaginary door to join her imaginary little friend. Or when she lay for months incarcerated in her plaster cast, staring at her own reflection in the mirror. After a while what she saw was not herself but a mask. Virtually all of her self-portraits show the fixed look of a mask. Masks were important to her, they hid the reality behind them. As with every actor, masks and costumes allowed her to become whatever she wanted to be. Her life with the Maestro soon became a play where she designed her own costumes and sets, scripted and staged the story, directed and starred. And then she put it all on canvas.

She would spend hours brushing her hair and dressing, turning routine into ritual. The costume, the makeup, the hair were all her way of holding herself together. And she had a sense of humor. It amused her to parade around with the Maestro, she loved all the acting and ruses. When she stood in front of the mirror in the mornings, deftly applying her bright red lipstick, she would immediately feel different, she would become a different woman. Like a skeleton decked out in fluttering brightly colored scraps of cloth.

The question that troubled her was: if illness makes you hate your own body, how can you expect anybody to love you? She believed she had found such a person and could not risk losing him. It was not just her ego. Except for her earliest childhood, her relationship with her body had never been simple. Her body was a painful burden, an object of medication. And later an object of her art. An instrument of vanity. And of pleasure, as well—but above all, it was an *object* and an *instrument*.

Once again, as when she was little and recovering from polio, she found herself in a situation where she could completely withdraw, hide her shortcomings and in doing so hide herself. Or she could draw attention to herself with her deliberately exotic look and make it popular and loved. She worked on being popular and loved. She made alliances, the helpless always make alliances. And so Lupe, yesterday's enemy, became her best friend. She saw any new woman within sight of the Maestro as a threat and tried to win her over. Like a viper, she would first hypnotize and then neutralize her with her charm. She would then paralyze her with her venom. Frida was afraid that the Maestro would then leave her and she defended herself any way she knew how.

In those days she referred to her painting as *dabbling, unimportant*, as if talking about a hobby like gardening or needlepoint. That way she risked nothing. Caught between art and survival, she chose the latter. Like all unwell people, she had a strong survival instinct and it kept her constantly on guard, even when there was no reason for it. It was the instinct of a woman who knew that she could not let the Maestro feel threatened. Don't bite the hand that feeds you, she thought, echoing her mother's warning. For a long time she hid behind a veneer of modesty, saying painting was just a "hobby" because she felt safest when she was, in the Maestro's eyes, merely a woman who painted as a pastime, for her own amusement. Exactly as Doña Matilda had imagined when she had given Frida her first paints and brushes. It suited her to maintain this image.

The Maestro supported her painting—as a friend, a patron, the way he supported his students. He took it more seriously than Frida did. He told her that she was a better portrait painter than many a famous artist, better than him, better than Picasso. He taught her not to imitate anyone, to be true to herself. He introduced her to the folk tradition of the small votive paintings in churches, a form she enthusiastically adopted. He recognized her talent, that *something* in her paintings that was personal, intimate, painful and completely individual and distinct. He knew how different they were from his own paintings. Devoid of ideology, history and politics, her paintings were powerful in a different way. But it never dawned on him that Frida could become his rival. After all, he was a world-famous artist and she was famous mainly as his wife.

He built for them two houses with a connecting bridge and she got her own studio, this talented little wife of his who claimed that she painted only to amuse herself, that it was nothing serious.

But there was another reason why she did not assert herself as an artist. It took her time to accept that the demon of pain was there to stay and that the only temporary thing about it was its sleeping pattern. She needed strength to accept this, to continue painting and not bury herself away and let herself be completely consumed by illness.

The Maestro was getting big commissions not only in Mexico but also in the United States, in Detroit, New York and San Francisco.

She went to the States for the first time. She was cold there. Her back was giving her trouble. The Maestro was working on a scaffold outdoors somewhere. She did not know what to do with herself in this foreign land. She was not used to being alone and she was afraid, especially at night. Illness had instilled fear in her. Back home in Mexico she was never alone, she had Kity, her parents, her other sisters and friends. Why had she ever come here?

Why did the Maestro not see that she couldn't live in America? Wasn't it obvious that she was unhappy being away (from herself, from her country), that she felt bad in the States? He, however, felt good. All he could see was his own needs, his own importance. He was courted by the elite of New York, even by rich industrialists, though he himself was a communist. The Maestro was a vain but pragmatic man; he saw nothing paradoxical or wrong about it. His American commissions brought in money and there was never enough of that.

Meanwhile, his exotically decorative wife—the flower in his buttonhole, as he liked to say—was melancholic, at times even depressed. More than anything else, she was nostalgic. Sometimes she wondered what she was spending her time on. On the Maestro, on friends. Was it a waste of time? Yet another question she had no answer to. She was still not sure that she was really a painter. She just knew that she wanted to paint and to sell her paintings in order to earn money and be independent. And that what she had become was the wife of a genius.

While he was painting his subversive, controversial, sweeping murals, Frida was sitting at home alone and, when her inner demon drove her to it, she would reach for her paintbrushes.

The small paintings she did at the time were unusual and suffused with pain. Though confessional, they were highly provocative because they cut through you like a knife. Even when not immediately decipherable, they had a visceral affect, they were like a punch in the stomach.

She came back from America with the painting My Dress Hangs *There. It had been snowing heavily in New York that winter and she had worked on this canvas in the gray light that spilled into the apartment through the tall narrow windows. She had added a touch of bright green to the dress hanging on the clothesline between the toilet bowl and the urn, against a backdrop of icy gray sea and, in the distance, the city. It looks so forlorn, this Mexican dress hanging there above the garbage and the smokestacks, the skyscrapers and the stock exchange, above the church spire with its dollar sign, the new god to whom Americans prayed, and, in the distance, the Statue of Liberty. Divested of a body, alone, lost somehow in this alien setting. Next to it in the background is a huge billboard with a picture of a film star, woman, or what Hollywood had turned her into. Not a living soul inhabits this painting. There is nothing strange about that. What is strange is that Frida is not in the picture. To anyone who knows her, this absence,*

*this relinquishment of self, comes as a surprise. Instead of doing
her usual—painting herself to confirm her own existence—she is
simply no more.*

She wanted to give the Maestro a child, but he already
had two children and was not all that keen on having a third.
She was still naïve enough to believe that a child would bind
him to her. Later she realized that this was not the only reason, that she wanted a child for herself as well. Women who
had children, she knew, were never so desperately lonely and
she thought that if she had a child she would feel less lonely
herself. Love was not a strong enough medicine to cure her
growing isolation.

One miscarriage, then another. The memory of it was still
vivid, like a nightmare: she wakes up, the sheet is drenched
in blood. She is alone. She cries, then she calls out for help.
They rush her to the hospital. Her body is lying on the operating table at the Henry Ford Hospital in Detroit. The glar-
ing lights bear down on her pale face, her eyes are closed,
beads of sweat glisten on her forehead. Her legs are spread
and raised on stirrups. She is still bleeding; pink, red and
purple roses seem to be blossoming on the blood-soaked
sheet under her body. The nurses are preparing terrifying-
looking instruments: needles, knives, clamps, scoops. Her
body is asleep and still. This time she will escape pain. Seated
between her spread legs, the doctor gets down to work. He
inserts the instrument. He holds his hand out to the nurse
and she gives him another instrument, his sleeves are stained
with blood. From deep inside the body of the sleeping young
woman, he removes the remains of the fetus. He scrapes the

dead tissue from her womb; no point in calling this clump of blood a child. This is her first miscarriage. Soon she will wake up in a cold sweat, feeling nauseous. She will vomit. Her gouged-out womb will continue to bleed for a while. She will feel as if it has been turned inside out.

She started painting *The Henry Ford Hospital* while still in the hospital. The Maestro brought her anatomy books and the doctor brought her a fetus in formaldehyde. The Maestro later told her that she had painted a masterpiece, that no woman had ever painted anything like it. If that was true, the painting had cost her dearly.

In her nightmares she saw her miscarried fetus floating in formaldehyde. Had they removed it intact after all? How big had it been? What sex? In another dream her unborn child was alive, floating, moving its tiny fingers and toes. It had blue eyes and laughed. But it was not a child, it was her favorite doll. The doll was dead. The child was dead.

She paints herself with the doll, a lamentation for the child she will never have. In Self-Portrait with a Doll, *she is holding the doll in her arms, she is not playing with or touching it, she is not even looking at it. The doll is no substitute for a child, just a reminder, a dead object.*

Frida is sitting on the little bed in the eerily empty room, next to the naked doll. She sits there staring, smoking. That is all she can do. She is as lonely as before. She doesn't expect anything anymore. She feels sad, empty.

After the miscarriage in Detroit, she saw death wherever she turned. Was there any way out of all this? she wondered. She contemplated suicide already then. But she knew that death was always there as a possibility. She, who had to fight to survive, saw death grinning at her with every injection, before every operation. It was always within reach.

Life, not death, still posed the greater challenge. She had to give birth to herself. To restore herself to life. To endure her life sentence with no chance of appeal. To live. If only she could explain to the Maestro how deep, how destructive this feeling of being *mute*, of being an *outcast*, was. Did he understand her, she wondered, had he ever understood her? Sometimes she thought that at some level he did. At other times it was as if they were speaking different languages, he the language of politics and ideology, which was what he saw as his reality, and she the language of emotions, pain and solitude. Male and female art? She didn't think like that. But she was aware of the difference between a man's experience of reality and a woman's, and even more between a sick and a healthy person's.

Sometimes, like an unstoppable force, her familiar demon simply had to break out. It looked for ways to do it. It used tears, cries, swear words. Only painting could quell or control it. Because when she painted, she felt released from her body. Her body simply became a medium. She would forget about it and about herself. And these precious moments of peace were her reward.

Her self-portraits would show her screaming from down a hole, calling for the Maestro. She had to believe in the possibility of communication between them. Because on the surface she was this cheerful, colorful person, this entertainer whom everybody adored and who hardly ever complained.

She discovered that painting self-portraits boosted her self-confidence. The principal difference between her "seductive" and her other self-portraits was the absence of self-awareness in the former and its strong presence in the latter. With time, she became brutally direct. In her later self-portraits she was no longer beautiful, merely odd-looking. She did not seduce, she simply drew attention to herself. Her face became hard, serious. The pronounced cheekbones and heavy eyebrows looked as if they had been carved out of stone. The stern black eyes looked either straight through or straight past the viewer. She deliberately exaggerated the brutality of her self-portraits. She was saying: Look at me, I'm alive and it hurts. These self-portraits were like attestations to her existence: one, two, three, four . . . Exhibitionism, they said. But for her, painting self-portraits was a kind of magical rite, a kind of exorcism.

She did not kowtow to popular taste and still less did she try to win over the public. Except for that first self-portrait, all the others were unsparing of both the sitter and the viewer. As if she did not care whether they would appeal to somebody or not. She painted her life, why should it appeal to anybody? She painted a faint mustache on her face, something any other woman would have bleached, plucked, shaved, concealed. She was out to provoke, and why not? Who says a woman can't sport a mustache above her scarlet-red lips? The Maestro was taken by her androgynous quality, he found this male touch on the female face attractive. Oh, men are subconsciously all homosexuals, it excites them to see those wisps of a mustache above a woman's lips, like on the face of a pubescent boy, she would explain cheerfully, as if tickled by the idea. Anyway, she knew that it made people stop and look. But it was not only the little mustache that was meant to grab people's attention, it was also the eyes, the face, the clothes, the whole person. It was yet another provocation, a way to make people not only stop and look but also see.

When even this was not enough, she resorted to a still stronger, crueler language. She painted a broken paintbrush, wounds on the leg, a carved-out heart, blood gushing from slashed veins, a body pierced with arrows, herself dead, herself planted in the earth. She painted fetuses and miscarriages, white bloodstained sheets and birth—legs spread open, an infant's head peering out. There was nothing gentle or sweet about the scream of the woman giving birth, about the cry of the child—she herself—being born.

She still had the sensation that death was shadowing her, hovering over her every painting. It was her job, she felt, to hold that shadow at bay, to master her fear of it, perhaps capture it in her paintings. The Maestro liked to say that painting was his life. She made no such declarations, but it was no less true of her as well. She would loudly denigrate her own paintings, but the truth of the matter was that painting was her life preserver; it kept her afloat and allowed her to swim, to breathe.

She was in Detroit when her mother died. Doña Matilda died unexpectedly, after a gallbladder operation, just when Frida was hoping that her mother would finally be rid of the insidious stomach pains, tension and ill humor that constantly plagued her. She thought it must be some kind of stupid joke, to die of such a banal, routine operation. She would have found it easier to bear if her mother had died of something life-threatening.

She herself had barely survived her second miscarriage. She had almost bled to death and was still recovering. She knew what it meant to lie on the operating table surrounded by cold walls and masked faces that later reappeared in her nightmares. She was all too familiar with that moment between the first intake of ether and the complete loss of consciousness, that moment when your vision blurs, when you gasp frantically for air in fear that you will never come back, but it just makes you slip into unconsciousness all the faster.

The last thing you remember before going under is that instinctive fear of not waking up. She knew every preoperative minute by heart and that part no longer frightened her, that moment when you cease being a person and become just a physical body—somebody's, nobody's—which has to be prepped. And that means putting the body on the operating table, strapping it down and covering it, then uncovering the section where a second later the surgeon will make his incision. She knew the cold touch of the iodine-soaked cotton, the smell that reached her nostrils and made her cough, the rustling of the sheet covering her, the muffled footsteps, the reflector lights being switched on. The voices talking about her in the third person as if she were already unconscious or dead. The eyes above the face masks covering the nose and mouth. The impersonal touch, the automatic movements of people who spend the entire day in this operating theater as one body replaces another. She knew that this was how Doña Matilda must have felt during those last conscious seconds of her life.

There was never time, we never had time for each other, she thought that morning in bed. We always think we will have time to say and explain everything to those we care about, to show how much we understand and love them. Sudden death is unfair to everybody, including those left behind. When we talked, it was always about sickness, food, other people. It was never about the two of us. Or about Father. So much was left unsaid. Had she lived, maybe I would have mustered the strength one day to ask her: Mama, why didn't you come and see me in the hospital after the accident, when I thought I was dying, when I was so alone and afraid of death?

The last time they saw each other, just before her trip to America, they had been arguing about the Maestro again. Doña Matilda could not stand him. She was unhappy that the two of them were leaving. She was convinced that the long trip would ruin her daughter's health. That nothing but cold weather, bad food and loneliness awaited her there. Doña Matilda could have said that she would go with them because it was better for Frida. But she merely commented cynically to Frida about how her artist, the famous communist, was off to paint murals for the capitalists, whose money didn't seem to bother him.

Your artist, that was how she referred to the Maestro, as if he were not a real artist, just someone her daughter had invented. Doña Matilda was sitting at the table, embroidering a pillowcase as she talked. Her face was drawn, paler than usual. She looked unwell, but unlike her daughter, she did not try to hide it. Her suffering was demonstrative, the only weapon she had against her husband and children. She used pity to get her way. You always believe what the newspapers say, you could show him some respect and gratitude at least, the man is supporting this whole family, Frida shouted, storming out of the house. It was always the same story with her mother, arguments, silence, reproach. It was pointless to try to talk to her, to try to win her love. And of the four sisters why was it she who had to make such an effort? she wondered, tears stinging her eyes.

She did not make it back to Mexico in time. She traveled from Detroit by train for days, but she did not make it. By the time she arrived at the hospital, her mother was already unconscious. She leaned over and kissed her on the forehead. Her mother opened her eyes and squeezed her hand. That was all. But Frida was not sure that she had recognized her.

After returning to Detroit she spent her days sitting by the window overlooking the street. From the fifth floor, people seemed to be rushing around, like characters in one of those silent movies that she liked to watch so much. Perhaps it was true, maybe people in the States really did move differently, faster. She sat by that window, her mind elsewhere, her body stiff. As if a part of her had died with her mother. I should have told you that I would miss you, Mama, she thought, distractedly tracing a door on the window with her finger. But she could not open that door anymore. There was no escape from the depressing, foreign room. She anguished over their unfinished relationship, over all the things that had been left unsaid between them. Her mother's silent worry. The silences with which she surrounded her daughter.

And the room, all the emptiness that engulfed her.

A succession of related illnesses turned into a lengthy, almost continuous test of endurance and pain. She was increasingly forced to concentrate on herself. She tried not to neglect them, but the people around her sometimes saw her behavior as selfish and egocentric. Yet she was simply trying to survive. How could she explain it to them? she wondered. How could she tell them that she had to make a supreme, unimaginable effort to do even the most mundane things such as getting up, washing, walking, sitting? Sometimes the pain was so bad she could not even sit. The physical effort it cost her was not something she could put into words, and it only became evident when she came close to collapsing. She thought it was her fault that others did not understand her. She blamed herself for pretending to be stronger than she was. The price of that was that people became used to seeing a strong woman, a woman who could do everything herself, who needed no help and even helped others. She enjoyed that, but the strain was often too much for her.

And when I couldn't go on anymore, when I had to show how weak I am, then they would accuse me of being selfish. Or of using my weakness to draw attention to myself. No, there is no compromise between the sick and the healthy, no real understanding. But by the time I realized that it was too late, she thought as her temperature rose. She watched the morning light creep in ever closer through the window.

Every morning she would check the state of her body. Carefully. She did not want to risk a sharp stab of pain. She would repeat the same movements, move and stretch in the same way, always cautiously, always afraid that the pain would seize her if she ever let down her guard. First she would move her leg. Then she would focus on her spine, from the nape of her neck to the small of her back, where the pain was usually concentrated. Sharp or dull, the pain tended to reappear right there, in her lower back. It was hard for her to give up this morning ritual, pointless though it might now be, because these routine, almost automatic movements were her only remaining connection with her body.

Suddenly she remembered another morning twenty years earlier. Another nasty shock when the two people closest to her had betrayed her.

It seemed like only yesterday:

First came the light. It crept slowly under her eyelids, warm and red like blood. It was like looking at herself from the inside, from under the skin where the blood courses through the veins and turns light pink at the touch of the sun. She still did not feel like opening her eyes. Sometimes her eyelids were her only defense against reality. Those two thin lids of skin allowed her to retreat even deeper into herself, to a place where no one and nothing could hurt her. She felt warm and safe that morning as she lay in bed, lulled into a kind of absence.

She knew what she would see when she opened her eyes. To the left of her bed was the night table and on it a tray with a little bottle of Demerol, a syringe, some cotton and alcohol. And a glass of water that Mayet had left the previous night before tucking her in, shutting the window and switching off the light. Tiny bubbles of air, like miniature transparent pearls, clung to the walls. There was a vase with a bouquet of wildflowers from the market, a pack of cigarettes and matches. On the table was a bowl of pomegranates fresh from the garden, and aligned on the white wall above it were photographs in dark wooden frames. To the right she would see the big curtainless window. And if she sat up and looked out the window she would see green trees. She was still not used to the second-floor bedroom and studio in the new house that the Maestro had built for her next door to his.

Her room in the new house was light and spacious, so different from the dark old room crammed with heavy furniture on the ground floor of her parents' house where she had grown up. Her eyes still closed, she reached for the syringe to kill the pain. She did that every morning; first the injection, then a cigarette, which she smoked in bed, waiting for the injection to work its magic. Only then did she embark on all the other preparations for a new day: getting up, washing, dressing, eating. Her fingers were already touching the syringe when she changed her mind. That morning she thought she could get up without Demerol. Her swollen leg wasn't hurting, though she knew that would probably change as soon as she stood on it. But she was prepared to risk it that day because she had woken up without her habitual corset or the dull pain it usually brought to her rib cage, making it hard for her to breathe.

The day before, she had had a visit from Dr. Velasco y Polo, the only doctor she trusted not to invent some new, even more painful instrument of torture, some new kind of corset. Finally, after a month, he had removed the cast. She inhaled, filling her lungs with air. She lay there like that, enjoying this wonderful feeling of freedom. This was how medieval knights must have felt when they removed the armor that confined their movements but protected them from certain death in battle. Free of the cast's constraint, she finally felt light, like a butterfly that had just shed the body of a caterpillar. Every time the procedure was repeated and she was free of a cast or some other body cage, it was like being completely released from her body. Suddenly she would feel incredible relief. This feeling of bodilessness would not last long, perhaps no more than a second, the blink of an eye. But the sensation was so strong that she thought it was almost worth wearing the miserable piece of armor if only to experience the joy of shedding it.

It must be wonderful to fly and not have to crawl like me, she mused that long-ago morning, not for the first time. The doctor examined the scars on her back from the last operation, mumbling approvingly, and she was already thinking how she would step into a tub of warm water and lie there submerged for hours just to prolong this feeling of lightness. Because her body would be almost weightless underwater. She ached not to feel her body, just the warm touch of the water. Healthy people must feel like that all the time, until something starts to hurt, she reflected. She was intrigued by the thought that basically *they don't feel* their body. And when they do become aware of it, it is usually a bad sign. It's discomfort or pain that reminds them of their body. Of course, it can also be pleasure, she mustn't forget pleasure. If she were healthy, her body would not feel like a locked cage. She would simply get up and walk, thinking about something else because her body would be in perfect working order and would not hinder her movements. Like the people around her every morning, like Kity, the Maestro, the children.

But only healthy people had the luxury of not thinking about their body. When you are sick all your life, you feel like a prisoner serving a life sentence.

Still, she was so happy that morning to wake up without the plaster shell and be able to breathe freely. She lit a cigarette, her eyes open now. She took a long drag, filling her lungs and letting the nicotine surge into her blood. This was another morning ritual, a sensual pleasure. She liked the smell of tobacco and the touch of the fine paper as she twirled the cigarette between her fingers and shreds of tobacco fell into her lap. Then the sun burst into the room and every object suddenly looked new. The colors seemed to scream as if they were alive. She had not vomited for two days, perhaps that was a small ray of hope for the baby she was carrying. It was her third attempt. The last time the doctor had said, This will kill you, don't get pregnant again unless you want to kill yourself. Frida was still hoping to have a child, she wanted to prove to herself that she could do it, but at the same time she was afraid that her body would again rebel against carrying such a burden.

She would tell the maid that she had decided not to have breakfast in bed this morning. She was free and would celebrate it by sitting at the table like any normal person, having her breakfast and leafing through the papers. Unless, of course, her sick leg interfered. It had started acting up again, but it was still bearable. She knew the pain would ease once she had the injection, but she would not be able to walk, or if she could, only, maybe, to the Maestro's studio in the other house. I have to prepare myself for the amputation of my toes, she thought. After one of her toes had literally fallen off she could not delay the operation any longer. She could not stop the gangrene by sheer force of will, which she had realized when she found a piece of black rotting flesh under the bandage. But she did not want to think about gangrene that morning.

Whenever she thought of that day twenty years ago, the first thing she remembered was how inexplicably cheerful she had been. She had spent almost the whole morning in the bathroom, with the maid helping her to wash because of her sick leg. Then the nurse came to change the dressing. It doesn't look too good, you'll have to do something about it soon, the nurse said, as if Frida didn't know that herself. Tomorrow, Frida replied, tomorrow I'll set a date with the doctor for the operation. Just not today, she thought, today I am free, free of the corset, free of my dark thoughts. She plaited and fastened her hair with the two new tortoiseshell combs the Maestro had recently given her. Then she had a cup of strong black coffee and a fruit salad. As she ate her breakfast she read the papers; the rise of fascism and developments in Germany that year occupied her attention.

Finally she set off for the Maestro's studio, slowly, leaning on her cane. She wanted to tell him how well she was feeling that morning, maybe she would even manage to keep the baby. She decided to tell him that even though she knew he would frown at the mention of her pregnancy, because he felt it was crazy to put her health at risk like that.

As if he didn't know that she always went for the impossible, for unnecessary risks, for insane stubbornness, for stretching her body to the limit.

Later she found it strange that she had had no premonition of what was to come that day, just as she had had none before the accident. She thought she knew how to read the signs, that she could sense when there was a new woman in the Maestro's life by the way he would avoid her eye, become jittery and be in a constant hurry. And by the far-off look in his own eye, and the unnaturally cheerful atmosphere at lunch. He would turn the conversation to politics to avoid discussing what was really happening between the two of them. Those were the Maestro's little tricks to make the atmosphere in the house more or less bearable.

She was also convinced that she could recognize a new mistress by her smell. When the Maestro would give her a wet peck on the cheek before going into his studio she could always tell if he was carrying the smell of another woman on him. But that day she failed to recognize the smell of her own sister Cristina, of Kity. Perhaps because she was used to it. Kity was always around and her smell was already intermingled with Frida's and the Maestro's. Or maybe, she thought later, she hadn't sensed it because Kity's smell was not yet on him. Maybe they had suddenly been overcome with passion for the first time that day, like a surging wave.

Kity often sat for the Maestro, who once even declared that she was his favorite model. And she was always there, a part of his life. But Frida wondered how and why Kity had become his mistress. How could the two of them disregard her like that when they must have known how much their double betrayal would hurt her? Maybe she had been unfair to Kity, she mused later, when she had blamed her for the affair. But what else could she have done? From the very beginning of their marriage, the Maestro had set great store by his freedom, as was evident from his behavior, and she had to get used to it if she did not want to lose him. She should have realized immediately that he, not Kity, had made the first move. Kity had always been a conventionally passive woman, and maybe that was what the Maestro found so attractive.

Yes, later she realized that she had accused Kity of seducing the Maestro and that she had done so instinctively. It lessened his responsibility for their betrayal and so she could justify him. She cared more about justifying the Maestro than about Kity. She could not risk losing his love, she could not survive without it. But she could survive without Kity, she thought at the time, though as the years went by she was not so sure. Kity had completely devoted herself to Frida since her back operation when her health had suddenly taken a turn for the worse. It was she, not the Maestro, who spent days and nights with Frida, keeping her company, entertaining, feeding and washing her, brushing her hair and enduring her abrupt mood swings. Did Kity do it because she felt guilty about her affair? she wondered. But that was all twenty years ago; did she still feel so guilty? She knew that she bore some of the guilt herself. Before Kity's affair with the Maestro, Frida had never doubted in her, never been jealous of her. She had never seen her as a woman, only as a sister.

God, how arrogant I was, she thought now, I was so certain that Kity couldn't compare with me in any way.

Body. Kity. Her sick body. Kity's betrayal. Eleven months younger, shy, withdrawn Kity. The mother of two children, Frida's adored nephew Antonio and niece Isolda. The only one of the four Kahlo sisters and two half-sisters to have children. No one, other than the Maestro, was as important to Frida as her little sister. She could not remember a time before Kity. They were like twins. Always together, though Frida dominated. Kindergarten, school, polio. Her obedient little Kity, who knew how afraid she was to be alone and was always there, comforting her when she cried, lying in bed with her until she fell asleep. They were inseparable until Frida was accepted at a prestigious secondary school. Don Guillermo thought that Kity, like the other two sisters, was "slow." Kity—green-eyed, fair-skinned, soft, round. And quiet and undemanding. Always under her thumb. She is everything I am not, Frida always thought. Yet, she found it perfectly normal that her younger sister should listen to her. And serve her. Did I miss something? she wondered when it was all behind her and everything had been forgiven. Yes, she had missed the fact that Kity was herself a beautiful, desirable woman.

Once she had dropped by the Maestro's studio when Kity was sitting for him. She was seated on a chair, nude and clearly already tired. She did not even try to cover herself up when her sister walked in. She's so beautiful, Frida thought tenderly. Her tummy was flat, her breasts firm; two pregnancies had had no effect on her looks. The Maestro was nervous, he could not paint quickly enough because Kity was tired of holding her leg up in the air in an impossible position. Frida's arrival cheered them up, they laughed and ate together, she and her husband and her naked little sister.

It was already early afternoon when Frida finally left her room for the studio that day long ago. She stopped in front of the door. It was ajar. She heard no voices, which usually meant that he was alone, working. She pushed open the door and walked in. At first she didn't see him. The Maestro was not hunched over his sketches at his desk, or standing in front of his easel. As she turned to leave, she caught sight of the bed in the corner. She could still conjure up the scene, as if she were standing in that same spot on the worn wooden doorstep of his studio. It was like remembering an all-too-familiar photograph.

Yet another picture I never painted, she thought, unexpectedly upset by the memory.

Lying naked in the bed was Kity. She had fallen asleep on her side, her legs pulled up, the way she used to nestle next to her as a child. Hug me, she would say back then. Frida would wrap her arms around her waist and hold her like that until she fell asleep. Years later, it was Kity who would hug Frida when she couldn't sleep.

She slept there peacefully, the afternoon light gently caressing her fair skin. She saw how *complete*, how perfect Kity's body was. From the doorstep her gaze fell on the white scar under her knee, the only small imperfection on Kity's body. She remembered how they had been playing in the park and Kity had asked if she could ride her bike. But she was clumsy and fell only a few meters later, cutting her knee. Frida had wiped the gravel and earth off her cut and removed a shard of glass from deep in her flesh. She remembered how sticky the blood had been on her fingers and how she had raised the transparent piece of green glass to the sun.

The Maestro was asleep next to her. He was naked as well. Kity looked like a fragile doll next to his big robust body. If he turns onto her side he will crush her, she remembered thinking.

For a while she just stood there, leaning against the doorframe, not moving, absorbing the moment and the day. As if Kity had died, images floated before her eyes: Kity holding her hand in the courtyard as Frida learned how to walk again, climbing into her sickbed with her, laughing and holding out her chocolate-smeared hand. Kity, her face bruised from her husband's punches, nursing little Isolda, feeding Frida soup with a spoon; Kity holding her hand in the operating theater as she went under.

The sky was blue, without a cloud in sight. Outside, she could hear men calling to each other and a dog barking. She could smell the paints, the linseed oil and something even more intense: the smell of their bodies. Observing them like that, she felt as if that shard of glass had now stabbed her somewhere deep inside. Used to pain, she let out the faintest of sobs.

The Maestro was the first to open his eyes. He was surprised to see her leaning against the door, but he did not seem upset. Lightly he touched Kity on the shoulder. She woke up slowly and turned toward him. Only then, following the direction of his gaze, did she see her sister. Kity sat bolt upright, wordlessly burying her head in her hands as if about to cry. She sat there, head bowed, face hidden, until Frida finally left, shutting the door behind her.

Now she looked around her again. For a while she watched the progress of the morning light, but the fever blurred her vision. A thin but opaque curtain, like the one that sometimes hangs around hospital beds, had already been drawn between her and others. Her gaze, even her voice and tears, her pleas and touch, no longer seemed to reach them. Hadn't it always been like that, she wondered, hadn't she spent her whole life enveloped in a membrane that was now become increasingly impenetrable? All she had left was random, unreliable memories. And her memory seemed like a fine cobweb. She still managed to hold her balance on the thin thread between two points, in the faint hope that she would eventually see the entire cobweb, that her life would turn out to have had a meaningful structure after all.

Her mind went back to that image of Kity's betrayal. She had seen her sister naked hundreds of times before. When they bathed in the tub together as children, when she had her first period, when they got dressed together. But that day it was as if she had seen her for the first time. She was lying in the bed, naked, beautiful—so much more beautiful than Frida. And so open to the touch of one's eyes, one's hands. Her fair complexion, her curves as if hewn from stone. For the first time Frida saw her sister through the Maestro's eyes, the eyes of a man and an artist. She was sure that to him Kity's body was a work of art. And she even understood why, in his yearning for harmony, he had reached for that body. He simply could not resist the challenge, she reflected when she had recovered from the sight.

But what she could not understand, at least not at that moment, was why her sister, her little sister, her protector and carer, had crossed the line. Unless, she later realized, that line had existed only in her own head.

Even before, she knew that the Maestro cheated on her. She did not call it cheating. When she was young she told herself that he needed the excitement of it, that he was an artist in constant search of sensations. And women threw themselves at him. They wanted to pose for him, to be immortalized in his murals. Sex with the Maestro was a shortcut to posterity. They offered themselves for even lesser gains, she was sure.

She would be infuriated. Offended. She could occasionally permit herself such emotions. But there was another, more brutal side to the story, one known only to her. Her wounded body could not always be at the Maestro's beck and call. She often spent months in the hospital, and even more often was exhausted or in pain. And so sometimes she felt as if it were she who was betraying him, she who was letting him down. One year, admittedly much later, she had seven operations on her back. She spent nine months in the hospital. She was helpless and in no position to demand that he be faithful, at least that was what she told herself.

And he consumed women the way other people ate their favorite fruit or ice cream. He did not change. But after the incident with her sister, something inside Frida changed forever.

She ran her finger absentmindedly over her dry lips. And over her teeth, as if counting them. She had ugly teeth, some of them were rotten. She remembered that her maid, who also had bad teeth, would cover her mouth with her hand when she laughed. So Frida mostly smiled. If she forgot herself and laughed, you could see her rotting, nicotine-stained teeth. She, who paid so much attention to every detail of her appearance, to the color of her lipstick and jewelry, to the kind of flower in her hair, neglected her teeth. If she had to worry about that on top of her sick spine, the wounds on her back, her rotting toes, well . . . It bothered her that nothing, not a single part of her, worked properly. Even her teeth were unhealthy. But bad teeth could be hidden. She concealed her withered leg under long skirts, her corset under wide shirts and her bad teeth behind a smile—and gold crowns. For special occasions she would wear the gold crowns inlaid with pink gems and then laugh with a wide-open happy smile. But it was easier to camouflage herself, to smile so that her teeth did not show. Willpower, camouflage, self-control, these were the guiding principles that helped her survive.

This restrained smile made her look softer in her photographs than in her self-portraits, though she was never completely relaxed in front of the camera. She was forever striking a pose. She was a good actress. She liked to look spontaneous, but in fact she believed in self-control. Hers was like a suit of armor that held her body together better than the detested corsets. Her willpower was what enabled her to survive.

Kity didn't need such willpower or physical effort to live her life. Frida had envied her that ever since childhood, when she was bedridden for months while Kity would run to the kitchen to bring her food, give her her toys, dance to amuse her. Frida, with her illness, had turned her sister, like everyone else around, into her servant. Kity's freedom of movement was something she had never had. Kity's body had not been disfigured by sickness or an accident, or even by childbirth. Yes, she had had two children, whereas Frida had had only miscarriages, each of which had been life-threatening. For this, if for no other reason, it was hard for her to get over what her sister had done to her.

Kity had good legs, good teeth, a smile—everything Frida did not have. So Frida had to make up for it, reinventing herself with the help of exotic clothes and strange hairdos, makeup and jewelry. She had to work hard at it, day in and day out. Kity had no such need, none at all. Plus, she was the only person who knew exactly how much it cost Frida to get up every morning, to wash and dress and walk. Still, she had shown no pity. She had betrayed her without giving it a second thought. Her betrayal was different from the Maestro's, but just as personal and just as painful.

You treat me as if I were stupid, her sister once told her later. He talks to me, he listens, you know? Unlike you, he treats me like a human being. But Kity had told her that at the wrong moment, when Frida still thought that Kity simply felt honored that the Maestro was finally paying attention to her. She was there, she was his model. Why should she resist the great Maestro when so many others hadn't? Frida could just imagine the scene, with him looking like a sad, forlorn child: I'm so lonely, Kity! And Kity comforting him. Women loved comforting him. He inspired in women both admiration and pity. He didn't care how he won them over. So why should this affair hurt her more than all the others, which she knew about, of course? Why, for God's sake, do you make a drama out of everything? the Maestro asked her.

The two of them were the closest to her, so close that they knew her every scar and every wound, everything she so carefully hid from everybody else. Never, she promised herself that day, never will I let anybody get that close to me again. It's life-threatening.

She still remembered that promise, impossible to keep, of course. Because she could not cut either Kity or the Maestro out of her life, it would be like self-amputation.

———

Kity's affair with the Maestro lasted at least a year. He bought her not only an apartment near their parents' house, but also a car. She would drive her father, her children and the Maestro, everyone except her sister. Frida behaved as if Kity did not exist. It was during this period that she had another miscarriage and her toes amputated: an empty womb, wounds, back pain and the feeling of having been completely abandoned.

The painting shows a naked stabbed woman with so much blood that it spills over onto the picture frame. She had dipped her brush in blazing red paint, too red for blood, and then had smeared it on the floor, on the shirt of the killer standing by the dead woman, his knife still dripping with her blood. The killer, a tough-looking macho character with a cynical smile, had one hand in his pocket and looked as if he were saying, So what, it's just a few little stab wounds. The woman's leg, with its elegant black shoe and stocking rolled down, looks grotesque, as does the deliberately exaggerated amount of blood. Maybe that is why the whole thing suddenly makes you want to burst out laughing.

Their fights—they were always lovers' quarrels—originated in their different approaches to love. This difference became apparent to her only later, after all her other relationships, not one of which lessened her affection for the Maestro or her suffering. She was not sure whether it was because he was a man, but art was more important to him than love. The most important thing to her was the Maestro. Which meant that she was bound to suffer.

She was twenty-seven when he cheated on her with her sister. The very thing that her mother had feared (and kept silent about) had happened, she thought. All of the Maestro's mistresses had one thing in common—bodies she could not compete with. At the time she thought that was why he cheated on her so often, and it hurt her. But her mother had been wrong about one thing. As much as the Maestro yearned, as an artist, for the possession of beauty itself—that harmony that her own body lacked—he longed even more for the freedom to possess any woman, regardless of what she looked like. Had her body been the picture of health, had she been as lovely as the actress Dolores del Río, the reigning beauty of the day, who (she knew) had been another one of his mistresses, it still would not have stopped him. But that she realized when it was already too late, when there was nothing she could change anymore.

For years I tolerated his affairs because I thought that his mistresses gave him something I couldn't—something physical, I mean. And for years they were famous beauties. I stopped trying to compete with them long ago. He finally stopped when Ema came along. She was anything but beautiful, but she had the patience and understanding the Maestro needed. Maybe I was wrong before, maybe he hadn't been yearning for harmony, for perfection. Maybe what he needed was simply a shoulder to cry on. So you've been reduced to Ema, I said spitefully. I was horrible to him, and even worse to her. Not because I had anything against poor Ema, who for years had worshipped him from afar, had sold his paintings in her gallery and probably suffered because he ignored her. No, I was horrible because I was bitter. I was miserable because, deliberately or not, he obviously took me for a fool. For almost all of those twenty-five years of marriage to him, I had lived in the conviction that something in his choice of women reflected the artist's yearning for perfection. Something that I, being as I was, could not be a part of. Something I tried to compensate for by resorting to all sorts of female tricks. What a waste of time . . . I took time away from my painting, the only thing I cared about, to make him love me, to seduce him, to be by his side.

I thought it was the kind of contest that somebody like me, brilliant maybe but ill, could never win. But I comforted myself with the thought (what else was left?) that the Maestro and I had something special together, that our relationship was so strong it could weather these passing threats. The fact was that the other people in our lives were not as important to us as we were to each other. Ours was a very special kind of love, I believed, where the other person represents your entire universe, one that fulfills you, one where you are not man and woman but *simply human beings*.

There was a period when, in desperation, every canvas I painted had the Maestro in it. As if I could cast a spell on him and keep him for myself.

There was no balance in our relationship. It was me who needed him, me who was always hungry, always wanting attention, wanting reassurance. In my world, he was the source of light and warmth. He was my food, my drug. He was my obsession. Why did I let myself become so utterly dependent on him? Because I was sick, I was vulnerable, I was weak.

She ran her tongue over her remaining teeth. Three of her lower teeth were missing. Plus two of her upper teeth, if she didn't count the two that she would have to have pulled (though she found it pointless to use the future tense). She had the feeling that they were all loose and that she could pull them out herself. She had been eating nothing but soup and pap for months anyway. It's awful how sickness reduces an adult to the level of a child, she reflected. Her teeth, like her bones, were older than her forty-seven years. She calculated that they must be twice as old because she had had to make twice the effort of a healthy person just to survive. So she was at least eighty, maybe even ninety-four. Suddenly she found the idea funny—she still hadn't lost her sense of humor.

After the incident with Kity, Frida moved out of the house the Maestro had built for her. She left him. She was sorry to leave the studio—she certainly could not complain that he hadn't respected her as an artist. After she had recovered from her third miscarriage and an operation on her foot, she found herself a lover, and then another; at some point she stopped counting or caring whether they were men or women. What mattered was the touch of the skin, passion. That was how she learned how to separate love (she called it love but it looked to her more and more like an addiction) from passion, something she was absolutely unable to do with the Maestro. From him she wanted both, but in their common universe insatiable passion was one-sided, her-sided. For Frida passion was a confirmation of his love. It was only when the incident with Kity happened that she realized the two were not necessarily connected. But she kept looking for excuses for him. Could it be, she sometimes wondered in despair, that people who have so much passion for their art in the end have none left for others? Or was passion simply a particular kind of energy that is not inexhaustible? Or was their closeness the problem? Could two people be so close and still feel passion? Finally, maybe her (excessive?) sexual desire was a reflection of her passion for life itself? But these were all questions that had troubled her even before the incident with Kity.

She took to serious drinking and returned to serious painting. She had to paint because the emotional pain she felt—which seemed to have settled like sediment on top of her old, physical pain—was too strong to contain.

She felt better when she was with a man; that was how she healed the wound the Maestro had inflicted on her. Her young lover, who knew both sisters well, described to her the difference between them: Frida had a fire burning inside her; Kity did not. And he told her, Only people who know death have such a fire.

She painted by day and went dancing by night. She had a need to outdo herself. So she danced. She liked this young man in his white shirt, with his rippling muscles, burnished complexion and finely chiseled face. As her body followed his lead in the dimly lit smoke-filled room, she could feel her desire for him grow. She would rest her head against his shoulder, press against him and inhale his smell, melting in his arms. Then he would slip out of her embrace. Quick and lithe, he would be lost in the crowd of dancers only to return to her. She would clasp him back in her arms until she felt the warmth of his body. They would fall into step. At that moment nothing was more important to her than his touch and her burning desire. I want you, she would whisper in his ear. This man made her feel alive, strong, desirable.

Later, when they talked about love, she told him, You are my lover but not my love. The young man looked at her and smiled. He was not bothered by her words. In the room that night she ran the tips of her fingers along his sleeping body, gently so as not to wake him. Young male flesh. I'm voracious, she thought. I want pleasure, I want my body to feel something other than pain . . .

Was it Frida's imagination, or had that bright ray of sun now dropped to the floor and started crawling in defeat as darkness reconquered the room? Or was it the fever blurring shades of light and dark? she wondered wearily.

Lying there in her bed at the break of day, she could feel only certain parts of her body now—the leg she didn't have, her teeth, face, hands, hair, heart. Heart? Her heart was still beating, she could feel it forcing the blood through her veins, but it had to work at it now. It was tired, this heart of hers which she had so often painted as lying wounded on the floor, in her lap . . . left ventricle, right ventricle, left auricle, right auricle . . . valves, veins, arteries. Anatomically it was a simple pump. In reality, her reality, the heart was a crushed, bloody, painful lump that trembled at the sound of its own voice, or at the absence of it.

She thought of the Maestro and how her living heart, her life, had trembled in his hands for so many years.

She needed time for a picture to crystallize. The colors were tiny crystals of pain deposited in her organism over time. They had to course through her bloodstream to the tips of her fingers. The hand would pick up a brush and dab at the paints. The brush would touch the canvas. So began the chemical process of moving the crystals to the canvas, resulting in the painting. After that she felt better for a while, as if her painting were some kind of primitive ritual to drive evil spirits away. Rituals, I can't live without them, she thought as she put brush to canvas. There is too much accumulated darkness inside me. How will I bear it?

In Self-Portrait with Cropped Hair, *Frida is sitting on a chair holding a pair of scissors. She has already chopped off the long silky mane that the Maestro loved so much and black locks of hair are strewn all over the floor. She is surrounded by chaos, chaos and a wasteland. The colors are dark, the atmosphere heavy and somber. Frida has discarded her long skirts and shawls, the peasant costume she wore for the Maestro. She is dressed like a man again. She is punishing the Maestro. Your Frida is gone, Frida is telling him in the picture.*

It hurts here, inside, she would say, pressing her hand against her breast. She drank a liter of brandy a day. After Kity, everything became complicated. Frida and the Maestro lived apart, but neither could do without the other. They continued to see each other every day.

She wrote to a friend:

We are living a lie, full of nonsense, and I can't take it anymore. First, he's got his work, it protects him from so many things, and then there are his affairs, which keep him amused. People look for him, not me. *I know that he's always got lots of worries regarding his work; still, he's living a full life and doesn't have my emptiness. I've got nothing because I haven't got him. I thought I was doing my best to help him live and that there was no situation in life that I could not easily solve. But now I know that I'm no different from any other disillusioned, abandoned woman. I'm worthless; I can't do anything; I can't live alone.*

My situation looks so ridiculous and pointless that no one can understand how much I can't stand myself, hate myself, I wasted my best years as a kept woman, doing what I thought was best for him and would help him most. I never thought of myself, and after six years together, his answer was that loyalty is a bourgeois value which exists only for the purpose of exploitation and economic profit.

She did not want the Maestro to support her anymore. She wanted finally to start earning her own money. Had money been the reason why, until Kity, she had tolerated the Maestro's sexual escapades? she began wondering. Lord knew there was never enough of it in her parents' house. It went for medicines, doctors, corsets, injections, nurses. After her accident she could never be sure that her father would have enough money and if he didn't, that her condition wouldn't worsen. Not long after Frida and the Maestro married, while they were still in Detroit, Frida's doctors told her that her spinal condition had deteriorated because she had not been operated on in time, immediately after the accident. Her parents probably could not afford yet another operation. They had already spent all their savings on her. Which was why she wanted to work, to paint and to sell her paintings. And then the Maestro came into her life. He took over the financial burden of her illness. She herself did not care about money, but she realized that she needed it. She wanted to have enough to feel safe. But she could not earn it by herself. She was completely dependent on the Maestro, as she realized when they separated.

In the fall of 1938 she was on her own in New York for the first time. On earlier visits she had simply been Mrs. Rivera, accompanying her husband. Young. Shy. There was nothing of the exotic, fascinating personality she was to become. But it was a completely different woman who welcomed to her exhibition the elite of New York and admirers of avant-garde art. Although some came because of the Maestro, after the exhibition they no longer saw her merely as his appendage. Her twenty-five paintings were different from anything they had ever seen before. She sold half on the spot and it boosted her self-confidence. She met new people, people who admired her and were charmed by her appearance and sense of humor. Finally she was on her own, successful and, she felt, free of the Maestro. "Little Frida" was how the critics referred to her after the show. A thirty-one-year-old woman, yet they wrote about her as if she were a child. But they also wrote about her paintings, and that gave her hope that she would finally become independent. That said, for an artist who was showing her work in the States for the first time, she was oddly indifferent to the reviews.

There was only one truly exciting moment at the opening that evening, she remembered, and that was when Georgia O'Keeffe appeared. She knew the American's work and her stylized, sexualized flowers. Julian introduced her to a woman wearing a long pale tunic and turban. She took Frida by the hand—her own was warm—and led her over to the painting *My Birth*. She stood there, looking at the painting. Nobody ever dared to paint this before. You've painted something that is never supposed to be seen, that nobody ever dares to witness because they are shocked by a woman's power to give life, she told her. The words gave Frida goose bumps. This woman could not know that they meant more to her than anything any critic, or even the Maestro, himself, might say. The woman's velvety eyes looked at her piercingly, as if they could see through her carefully arranged mask, through the layers of colorful clothes, through the corset, through her very skin. When Georgia, not accidentally, kissed her lightly on the lips, she trembled. Not with desire, but from instant recognition. Frida felt that after just one look at her painting, this woman, whom she had never met before, had shown a level of understanding that she had always dreamed of.

Stunned by the realization that something like this was even possible, if only briefly, she looked at her own painting as if seeing it for the first time. Just then Julian Levy, the gallery owner, came up to her, himself enchanted by both her and her paintings. And then somebody else came along, telling her something about her work, but it didn't matter anymore. All that mattered was that fraction of a second when another person had completely understood her.

That evening she circulated among the crowd as Frida Kahlo, the artist. Alluring and interesting. And for the moment, the pain was mercifully dormant, she realized. Her demon was asleep, quiet, deceived.

By the next day she could hardly walk. A wound had opened on the heel of her foot. Just enough to remind her that she was not alone, that there were two Fridas, one visible and the other hidden, surfacing only in her paintings. So she preferred sitting in cafés, observing people. She could not escape from herself, from her illness.

She spent her days with Nick Murray. She had met him in Mexico and ever since she had missed his voice, his hands, his laughter. She wrote to him that their love was so beautiful and real that it made her forget her pain and her problems, even when he was far away. I'm so close to you that I can hear you laugh, she wrote.

Nick would develop his photographs in the studio while she listened to music. Or he would take pictures of her. Standing behind the camera, he reminded her of her father, slightly crouched, his head under the black piece of cloth, only his arms and legs showing. He looked like a monster, half man, half machine. Like Nick, when taking photographs Don Guillermo used to require peace and quiet, as his daughters giggled, arranged themselves and got ready to have their picture taken "for posterity," as he liked to say. Look serious now, this is a photograph for posterity. That word, *posterity*, bothered Frida, and for a second she thought she would tell her father, but then she changed her mind. What could she tell him? That posterity doesn't exist. That only the present moment exists, the mingling of bodies, his words, the lingering smell of mothballs in the man's suit she had borrowed, the touch of her sister's dress, the anticipation. I've been there and back. Believe me, there is nothing, she thought as she stared fixedly into the lens of her father's camera. But she said nothing. She was already too aware of the powerlessness of words.

As Nick took his photographs, she smiled in the direction of his Cyclopean eye. She was wrapped in a cyclamen-colored shawl. Those lovely long fingers of his, I love their gentle touch, she mused, her eyes half closed, as if melting in his arms. And his thin, spindly body lying alongside mine. Nick watched her through the camera's eye. Don't move, he said. And she stood there, daydreaming for one more moment. The camera caught a trace of that dreamy, happy smile, a smile that never appeared in her paintings.

The light that illuminated her face that day was evanescent and soft. Nick was a master of lighting. A prince of lighting, she had called him the very first time she saw his photographs back in Mexico. He was a good-looking man, with a long face and regular features. She loved the gentleness of his voice and his movements. She found it easy to pose for Nick's camera. She looked at him with yearning. She opened her shawl as if she were about to surrender to him. The shawl slid down her smooth skin, baring her neck and shoulders. Its cyclamen color gave her face a brightness that seemed to dispel the dark hardness of her eyes. He abandoned his camera for a moment and walked over to embrace her. The music and the plaintive voice of the singer wafted out onto the terrace of the studio. Nick kissed her tenderly. Too tenderly, she thought; she wanted more than that. Why don't I ever have enough of tenderness or passion, she wondered, even at such a moment of perfect intimacy?

Again she saw her father in his studio, all those years ago. He was laughing at her suit, at the pose she struck of an arrogant young man with bold eyes. When he had finished taking the photograph, Don Guillermo walked over and patted her on the shoulder, shaking his head. What a marvelous idea, he said, to dress up as a man for the photo. They were both amused and for a moment the father forgot how sick his daughter was. She made it easy to forget. Out of the corner of her eye she noticed that Doña Matilda disapproved of her little ruse, and that saddened her.

Disturbed by the memory of her frowning mother, she pulled her shawl back around her shoulders. You don't have to hide, Nick called out from under the black cloth. Relax! She wrapped the shawl around her even tighter. She curled herself into a ball, like a porcupine, as if waiting for Nick to hurt her. Some words had that effect on her. Why had he used words that she hated, that made her have doubts? No, she could not be sure even of Nick. She could not relax and give herself to him completely because she knew that he could hurt her too much. Suddenly she was sorry that she had harbored any hopes. She had let him get too close, she knew that she was repeating the same mistake. He'll leave me, she thought sadly, as if his all too tender kiss already carried the bitter taste of his withdrawal and her pending defeat.

Soon after her return home, Nick sent her a letter confirming her worst fears. Her hands shook with fury as she read it. Fury at herself. I should have known, she thought. The woman in her was crushed, she had again been rejected by a man she cared for. Later, she replied and wrote him one last letter. It was friendly, as if there had never been anything between them. Or if there had, it had been nothing more than an insignificant affair. That was her revenge.

Her decision to live on her own and be independent was short-lived. Her paintings were not selling and her illness cost money she didn't have. Her impoverished parents could not help her. Though she had sold the paintings from her New York show and her reputation was growing, that still did not pay the bills. There was nothing for it, she had to rethink her decision and, as so many times before, adjust to the situation.

She had managed to live without the Maestro for a year. Now she went back to him. She told him she had forgiven him. He had never loved anyone the way he loved her, he said. She did not believe him. They were back together again, but things were not the same between them. She also forgave Kity, because she could not do without her, though she was not sure that *forgive* was quite the right word for what she felt.

She painted self-portraits with her hair down. After María Félix, her loose hair became one more symbol of sadness. The Maestro liked it when she wore her hair up like a crown. But the crown had fallen and her long hair wrapped itself around her neck, almost choking her. She thought how really she should not be painting herself but trains, two trains moving alongside each other on parallel tracks, never meeting. She tried to remember the moment when their lives had started moving in different directions, when the one no longer recognized shades of behavior in the other because no one was paying sufficient attention. But she could not pinpoint it.

Maybe there had never been such a moment. Maybe they had lived that way from the start, she just hadn't realized it.

She stopped trying to compete with other women for his affections. To make the situation more bearable, she reverted to her old tactics. She made friends with María Félix, just as she had already done with the Maestro's ex-wife Lupe, with Carmen, Lola, Paulette, Dolores . . . This was how she neutralized them. There were new ones, of course, but after Kity, Frida had no strength left for finessing. The pain in her back made it hard for her to sit, and sometimes even to lie down. No matter how many different kinds of corsets she tried they were all uncomfortable, they were too tight, they made it hard for her to breathe and sleep. Her leg did not get better even after her toes were amputated. All the same, she thought, the Maestro was still there somewhere, still nearby.

She dreamt, not for the first time, that she had broken out of her cocoon and flown away. That she had finally shed her body, like a butterfly. And then she realized that it was possible for even a human being to be free of its body. She would break the vicious circle of body-cheating-jealousy by ceasing to share the Maestro's bed. She told him that there would be no more sex. Their relationship transcended the body, she told him. Why torture herself and him? The Maestro himself had told her often enough that sex meant nothing to him. If it was true that he had never stopped loving that invisible side of her, she said, then it would be easy for him to ignore the physical part. When he asked her to marry him again, she said, All right, but remember, I don't want you in my bed. He agreed. A bit too quickly, she thought later. But regardless of her suspicions, she was relieved by the new equilibrium achieved in their relationship.

As they grew apart, the Maestro seemed to get smaller and smaller until he became a child whom she could cradle.

And so it was that her husband, an adult man twenty years her senior, gradually became the son she had never had. The Maestro himself was aware of this change, perhaps even before she was. In his mural *Dream of a Sunday Afternoon*, he depicted himself as a twelve- or thirteen-year-old holding the hand of Lady Death dressed in an elegant robe and plumed hat. And he also painted Frida embracing him maternally. In this portrait, there was nothing incidental about her hand on the boy's shoulder.

What the Maestro would not or could not verbalize, he expressed, as did she, in his art, in his frescoes. Although the scenes he painted were not intimate, she knew how to read them. For instance, she knew from the way he positioned a woman in his painting and certain other details—how he painted the eyes, for example—which of his models had been his mistress.

After Kity, she lost all interest in his love affairs. She stopped making scenes. Her illness was such a good, such an obvious, excuse for his unfaithfulness. But she despised him for being unable to control his sexual urge, and that was a new element in their relationship. If there was one thing she hated, it was the loss of self-control. She saw it as a mortal sin. The Maestro, on the other hand, detested self-control.

Sometimes, when she was wracked with doubts, she would accuse herself of being selfish. When you're in love, the other person's happiness is more important to you than your own, she thought. The Maestro—of this she was sure—had not stopped loving her, if love meant caring and support. Except his notion of love did not rule out relationships with other women. Relationships, that's what he called them. The one does not rule out the other, he would say. This was not the first time she'd heard him say something like that and she disciplined herself to get used to it and not hold it against him. Even after she found him with Kity, she began wondering why she should deny her to him, wasn't his pleasure more important to her than her own? Moreover, it was only now, when they were free of the physical part of their relationship, that they could achieve that spiritual union of which she had once dreamt. At such moments she would see the full paradox of the situation where, as a result of her sister's betrayal, her own relationship with the Maestro was entering a different, more elevated phase.

She still yearned for him. He continued to fill her world—whether from fear of abandonment and poverty, or because she sought an impossible love, it no longer mattered. She preferred not to analyze her motives; she was afraid of what she might discover. Meanwhile she had become even more aware of what an obstacle the body posed—her own and other women's—an obstacle that had always been there but had now turned into a wall she could no longer scale.

And so she was forced to find a different form for their relationship. As if love were a liquid that could easily be decanted from one vessel to another, she found a way to funnel the love of a woman into that of a mother. It was a painful choice, but probably the only one she had. And because of her self-discipline, she did not find the shift too difficult. The essence was the same, the warmth, the feeling of closeness and dependence too.

And so was the desire for possession.

In The Love Embrace of the Universe, *the Maestro is the center of her universe. She depicts him as a big, happy baby cradled in her lap, as if to say that this is his true measure. She is the mother who rocks him, takes care of and protects him. The Maestro is lying there naked and exposed, helpless. There is something grotesque if not perverse about depicting the Maestro, an adult man, as a child. She is holding her husband in her arms, and that husband is an infant. And he is reveling in the comfort and safety of her embrace. She asks nothing more of him than to be there, to rest in her lap. That makes her feel safe: he will never leave her—her little boy, her poor little frog. It fills her heart to cradle him, the way it would, she thinks, if she had had a child.*

Painting was no longer a "hobby" of the great Maestro's young wife. It had become a burning need, a way to survive his betrayal and her own new role. Just as the accident had changed her life, so his betrayal with Kity triggered a change in her attitude to painting. She was grateful that it had given her a chance to take things more seriously.

She had to paint; she couldn't keep screaming with pain.

There was a time, long ago it seemed to her now, when she had wanted to be as strong as the Maestro. She once wrote that for her he was "like a cactus that grows everywhere, as easily in the sand as among the rocks. And when it blooms, its flowers are a magnificent red, translucent white or sunlike yellow. It's covered in thorns to protect it . . . Its stem is strong even though it grows in hostile terrain, and its roots penetrate deeper than anxiety, loneliness and sorrow."

But she was not strong that way. Her defense mechanism was different. It was geared to protecting her from sickness and pain. The Maestro was able to *exclude others*, even when they were present. She sometimes hated this ability to live only for himself (for his art, he would tell her), to subordinate everybody else to his needs without even being aware of it. She called this self-focus indifference. But there was another word for it: self-centeredness.

How could she resist him? His magnetism was like the sun, drawing other planets into its orbit. She was not free, she had not broken away. She depended on him, on his strength, on his ability to earn money, to pull her out of her depressions, to take care of her. She needed him more than he needed her. She was insatiably lonely, capable of consuming all possible attention and affection and still feeling hungry.

A painful body, an unwanted body. I suffered on both counts. I was not only in pain, I had been rejected as well. However hard I tried, I never quite managed to separate myself from my body. I never succeeded in becoming a butterfly. How much easier it would have been for me if only I had believed in God and in devil, in heaven and hell, in the immortality of the soul. But after the accident I knew that my soul depended solely on my body, on this sarcophagus from which there was no escape. You can free me from this terrible captivity, I told the Maestro, by imagining that my body is not an obstacle to my soul. Love me, please love me. I begged him for love, any kind of love.

One day, I remember, the Maestro sat by my bed and took my hand. It was after one of my back operations and once more I was immobile. I looked at his cheerful face, his big eyes and open smile. He was in a good mood; he always was when his painting was going well. He smelled of turpentine, his hands were stained with paint. Imagine, he said, I've fallen in love again. Really? Again? I asked, failing to mask the cynicism in my voice. He noticed it. Just a little, he quickly corrected himself, winking to show he was only kidding. He was not kidding. The girl used to be a model and I need a few models for my new fresco, he explained. Of course, what else? I thought, saying nothing. When she first appeared I didn't find her interesting at all, the Maestro went on. Her face was too bland, I was about to turn her away. But when she undressed! That body! If only you could have seen it, he said, tracing her figure in the air with his big, strong hands. There was something naïve, almost boyishly excited, about the way they conveyed the beauty of the girl. It's as if he's talking about a magnificent, beautiful animal, was my first thought.

I had not met her but his gestures and enthusiasm sufficed for me to imagine her. I could almost see her standing naked in front of him. And him looking at her. And what I saw was terrible. Because it had nothing to do with beautiful animals.

I stopped myself from imagining anything more, I had to, otherwise I would have seen Kity in his bed again. And that would have hurt too much.

As the Maestro kept talking, I felt a mixture of sadness and joy. I was hurt by his cruelty in describing the young girl's body. The wound from my operation started to throb with pain. But we were together again and he had confided in me. That old feeling of insecurity returned: Was it the man in him talking or the artist? Or both? I didn't want to know. It was less painful that way. I knew that when he spoke about his fascination with the perfect body he was really talking about his fascination with *beauty*. He admired beauty and harmony wherever he encountered it and in that we were the same. But unlike me, if given half a chance to possess such beauty, he would not think twice about seizing it.

Listening to him talk about the girl, I realized that the woman in me was invisible to him. I heard the voice of this invisible woman, I heard her words, my words: My darling child, how I love you. My voice did not lie. It was the voice of a woman who had finally accepted her situation. At that moment I hated my maternal acceptance of the Maestro, that unconditional acceptance of anything my adored child did.

It hurt me to deny my femininity. I had acquired a child but lost a man. As he confided in me—stories he would never have told his mother, but we were also each other's best friend—the Maestro was finally content. I told myself that the definition of our relationship was less important than the fact that we both accepted it, that for both of us it was a way to stay together.

I longed for complete mutual acceptance and this was the only way to achieve it. I can still remember the warm touch of his hand taking mine that day. I fit so neatly into his hand, I hid and crouched there in the dark, not moving, not breathing. I longed for his touch, for the touch of a man, not a child. I longed for him. But I had to control this longing and turn it into something else.

The Maestro grew increasingly dependent on Frida, on her smile of approval for his love affairs. The smile of a mother. She loved him with that understanding, that all-forgiving love that everyone dreams of, that she herself dreamed of. They had achieved loyalty, which to her was perhaps the most important of all. She was sure that nothing more could derail their relationship, no betrayal, be it his or hers.

At their second wedding, in San Francisco, Frida was a different woman. The word *love* was simply a common term for their mutual dependence. Her terrible fear of loneliness had brought her back to the Maestro. Without him she would have been unable to bear the abyss of her illness. She simply could not be alone.

No one can live alone with pain, it is impossible.

But she no longer saw herself as just his victim. Obsessed with the Maestro, who remained the object of her admiration and possessive desire, she thought she had found a way to fulfill that desire without letting her obsession destroy them both. If the Maestro was self-centered, she was possessive, and increasingly aware of it. She wanted him for herself and this desire overtook all others. If I can't have your body, then I want your soul, she would tell him. But you already have it, he would say, laughing at what he called her "mystifications." She was not big-hearted. She was selfish because she had been hurt and had not found a way to avenge herself. She directed her sexual desire elsewhere.

What was left was a hunger, an emptiness, as if something big and important were missing. The unfulfilled need for love ruled her life like a cruel god. No one could give her this love, because it was unconditional. Not even her mother had loved her like that. Only her father, perhaps.

The light of day was growing stronger. She used to be afraid of the dark, but now she did not like so much light, the sharply delineated surfaces, the absence of shadows. Or perhaps it was the explicitness of this visible world. She found sun-drenched mornings especially cruel, the way the day devoured the last remnants of the night in the corners of the room. She had nowhere left to hide. The whiteness of the walls hurt her eyes. White, like the blanks in her memory. These crumbs of memory are the lingering fragments of my awareness, thought Frida. And they will vanish, the light will bleach my memory, like photographs dipped in the wrong liquid.

She took a sip of water and held it in her mouth for a moment, but she could no longer taste it. It could just as easily have been milk or tea, she had no sense of taste. That is gone too now, she thought sadly.

She dabbed cool water on her brow and temples. She could feel her temperature rising, her whole body starting to shiver. With a trembling hand she returned the glass of water to the night table. For days she had been alternating between feverish spells and restless sleep.

She dreamt that she was smiling, wearing a long white nightgown, her hair loose and arms open wide as if welcoming someone. Just as she was leaning down to take someone's hand she woke up. In a white nightgown, her hair loose, her arm reaching out.

In the last three years alone she had tried twenty-eight different kinds of corsets: plaster, plastic, iron, leather. The corset was a cage, and this was no metaphor, a cage constructed especially for her body. Without it her body would collapse, the flesh would sag and the bones scatter, she would not be able to sit, let alone stand. She was patient while they took her measurements, fitted the corset and tightened the screws, stretching her spine with the aid of small sandbags or suspending her from a special device hoisted onto a beam. She was patient while she waited for the plaster on her corpse (not body) to dry. She believed the doctors when, with each new, more modern corset, they told her that she would be better. She agreed to everything, striking bargains with herself, never complaining. But she had little hope that she would really get better, merely that she would continue to exist.

And even there, there were limits. To go beyond those limits, to suffer until the bitter end, waiting for death to take pity on her, seemed more like cowardice than an act of courage now. No one could accuse her of giving up easily. Thirty-two operations (maybe more, she wasn't sure, her counting was not as accurate as it used to be) were proof enough that she had fought for her life as long as she thought there was a point to it.

But being reduced to just breathing, swallowing and a beating heart was simply waiting for death to strike its final blow.

Had the Maestro pitied her from the start? The very thought brought a bitter, thick lump to her throat that she simply could not swallow. It was a doubt that sometimes plagued her, and she did not want to dwell on it.

Because, if that were so, then what made her relationship with the Maestro any different from her mother's and father's? Had Doña Matilda thought of her husband as weak because he suffered from epilepsy and was a shy, overly sensitive man of artistic temperament? Had she felt mostly pity for him, devotion, responsibility for a helpless human being? That did not preclude feelings of warmth and affection, but nor did it rule out the cold distance that prevailed between her parents. Her mother had suffered. Perhaps she had expected something else, something more. Like any woman. Like Frida.

Even if it had not been the starting basis of their relationship, with time the Maestro's love for her turned to pity. There was always an inequality, a gap between them that she tried to fill with whatever she could think of. She knew this because of the disbelief and gratitude she had felt from the very start, feelings she had never completely lost. What else could a cripple like her feel except profoundly thankful that anybody still wanted to look at her? At first it would fill her heart and bring tears to her eyes just to watch the Maestro asleep by her side. I must never, never let him go, because who knows if I will ever be able to find something like this again? she thought at the time. And she needed someone strong to hold on to, so as not to drown. The Maestro was as sturdy as a rock. If you want to be here, in this world, Frida told herself, then hold on to this man and never let him go.

She wondered whether their great and, she had long believed, cosmic love had grown out of her need and the Maestro's pity. She had built a myth around that love. Because in a situation where illness was consuming her piece by piece—while she fought back as she had when she was a child when her feverish mind thought a dog was trying to bite off her leg—she could not risk losing even a shred of whatever feeling he might have for her.

But she knew from experience that every illness feeds on pity and thrives on self-pity. Understandable though that might be, this was an emotion she allowed neither herself nor others.

But what if his pity was all there was—was even that too little? Yes, I wanted more than pity, I felt I deserved more than that. Of course, the Maestro's pity was not enough when it had to compensate for a bad leg, soothe the pain and make me feel whole and normal. But since it could not do that, and since his love did not have the power to make me whole and normal, I found a way to be special—out of desperation, not courage. I was not even an ordinary invalid, I was a walking freak show. A mustachioed woman with a flower garden on top of my head, dressed for a circus parade. No wonder children in the States cried out, Where's the circus?, when they saw me.

Like my leg brace, aesthetics, and especially the exotic, served me well. I was a good actress. Except everything visible in my life was false. My spouse was not really my husband but my child, and our grand love was just a myth. I needed strength to paint all that.

My paintings were a guide into the world of show and duplicity. Painting was the only safe place for me, a place of truth, a refuge. The only place where I could really be myself.

Suddenly her own lies and self-delusion made her sick. Before, she would have been humiliated by the mere thought that the Maestro felt pity for her, she would have dismissed such feelings as unworthy, as beneath her. But they were still feelings . . . and she could never get enough of that. At the same time, she convinced herself that she was the giver. What a delusion for someone whose very clothes, paintings, face were positively screaming for people to pay attention to her, her, her . . .

She was sick of herself. Death must come as a relief when you can't stand yourself anymore, she thought.

She thought of her father and how much she had missed him all these years. They had had illness in common and the same kind of loneliness that illness breeds. Don Guillermo had died of a heart attack, but she was convinced that he had died because he could no longer stand his own body or indeed himself.

She saw what happens when your body gives up on you. They had been in town when her father collapsed on the sidewalk right in front of her. It happened without warning, like being punched in the stomach or hit by a bullet. He was suddenly flat on his back, foaming at the mouth. His whole body was shaking violently as his bony hands tried to claw the air. She could not have been more than nine or ten years old at the time. She stood there beside her father, certain that he was dying before her very eyes. She was so terrified that she could not breathe and thought she would faint.

She recognized it as the mysterious illness that sometimes took hold of him, usually at night. When he had a seizure, Doña Matilda would worriedly send the girls off to the opposite end of the house and close the bedroom door. And when Frida would ask what was happening her mother would wave the question away and say it was nothing terrible, just one of his attacks. What kind of attack? Who had attacked her father? Those were questions her mother never answered. And she found it even more confusing when her father would appear at breakfast the next morning looking perfectly normal, calmly sipping his coffee and reading the newspaper as if nothing had happened the night before.

Now that same man, her father, in his white shirt and elegant suit, with his gold watch chain and silk tie, was lying on the dusty sidewalk in front of the paint store. Like an old drunk, she thought, flinching in shame that she could even think such a thing. She leaned over him. Daddy, Daddy, what's the matter, tell me what's wrong! It flashed through her mind that she was now uttering the same words to her sick father that he had used when the demonic pain had first attacked her leg. However, her father didn't hear her. His eyes were wide open, but only the whites showed. Suddenly she started trembling. She leaned against the wall. She stood there shaking, with clenched teeth and clenched fists.

People started gathering around. A man came out of the pharmacy across the street and patted Frida on the head. Don't be scared, little girl, he'll be better in a jiffy, he said. Then he leaned over her father and put something under his nose, but she could not see what. The convulsions stopped and her father slowly picked himself up off the sidewalk, took out a hankie and wiped the thin trail of spittle from his mouth. He dusted off his suit and took her by the hand. Without a word. Somebody asked, Do you need a doctor? There's one here nearby. Don Guillermo simply shook his head and proceeded to walk down the street. His pallor betrayed him, though. They walked home in silence, broken only by the sound of their footsteps. She didn't dare ask him anything, and he offered no explanation. His secret had been laid bare before a crowd of unknown people, and before his child. As he picked himself up off the ground he had seen not only fear on her face, but also shame. He knew what his convulsing body must have looked like, and the shame his little girl must have felt. He hugged Frida, whispering to her, Don't be scared, I'm fine. She nodded. She knew that her father was not fine and she felt helpless.

The next time her father prepared to go off on a photo shoot, Doña Matilda called the little girl into the bedroom. She took a small vial from the dresser and gave it to Frida. Take this with you and if your father collapses again, just open the bottle and put it under his nose. It's got alcohol inside and as soon as he smells it, he'll feel better. And watch out that nobody steals his camera, she added in the same breath. That was how she learned that her father suffered from epilepsy. She knew from her own experience that every illness carries with it shame, and this one, as she had seen for herself, was all the more shameful because it could strike anywhere, at any time. And there was no way to hide it.

Frida took the little bottle and carefully put it in her pocket. Scared though she was, she felt a certain amount of pride in the fact that her mother had placed her father in her care. She could not shake the memory of his contorted face and his eyes rolled up with only the whites showing. But even worse was the realization that her father, a grown-up and head of the family, could lose control over his body like that.

We never talked about my accident, Frida thought. But he was the only one who knew how I felt. He knew what awaited me and he was devastated . . .

She could sense Don Guillermo withdrawing into himself. His illness was something he felt he had to hide whatever the cost. It was because of it that he had dropped out of university in Germany, because of it that he lacked the stamina to cope with everyday life. He left all the important decisions to his wife. She raised the girls, took care of the house, saw to the maids, to the food, to the guests. Frida's accident only exacerbated the situation. He never really recovered from it. In order to survive and protect himself somehow he set various rules, which he followed to the letter: he had to eat alone at a certain hour and then would withdraw to his room and play the piano, again alone. Only certain compositions, though. Then he would read only certain books. Lights in the room were out at ten p.m. Strict rules, restrictions which he imposed on himself—like a corset, she thought. Otherwise, his life would have collapsed like a broken column.

The difference between us was that I was stronger. I wrestled with my demon by stripping him bare, revealing him, denouncing him. I was ruthless. I wore my illness down, sucked it dry, exploited it. I stubbornly resisted it. I lived in a state of permanent inner tension, waging a life-or-death struggle. I dragged my pain from its depths and brought it to the surface, exposing it to the light and to public scrutiny. Demons hate that. I displayed not only the face of that pain but also the body, its legs, its wounds, its heart, its stomach, its spine . . .

And that gave me strength. My rebellion was scandalous because not only did I paint, but I painted pain and sickness! Sick people don't do that. And my father? He sank deeper and deeper into his solitude. Toward the end, it was difficult to pull him out of it. I, on the other hand, refused to accept the sentence pronounced on me.

Did people pity me the less for it—or perhaps the more?

She wondered what her gentle father would have said. He was melancholic and, had he had the strength, he would have run away someplace where nobody knew him and nobody could bother him. Maybe even into the arms of death, had he had the strength for it. Her father, she knew, would have understood why she had to escape from her body, from a life that was nothing more than humiliating, unadulterated endurance. And collapse. Her life had collapsed like a broken column.

She remembered how miserable she had been when she painted that picture. It was not just her illness, because illness is more than mere pain, it is everything that surrounds and results from that pain. Like nails hammered into her naked body. She could almost identify all fifty-six of them: melancholy, loneliness, exhaustion, feebleness, resignation, unhappiness, misery, despair, fear, longing . . . She couldn't bear it all, she thought despondently.

She could feel herself falling apart. She painted a stone column in place of her spine. But even the stone was crumbling. The column that had held Frida up was now collapsing under too heavy a burden. I can't bear it anymore, Frida is saying in this painting. Her disintegration began ten years before her death, but here it is still an internal process, visible only in her paintings. The body is still whole, though laid open like on an operating table. For the first time she paints a body, sliced almost in half, like two shanks of pork. The dissected flesh gapes open. It is terrifying to look at. The running wound is deep and bloody. It is no longer even a wound, it is a tearing gash. The body is like the cracked arid earth in the background, longing for rain. There is a device artificially holding it together. But nothing, not this contraption or any of the operations, medicines, injections, can stop the general disintegration. The column cannot be repaired, the wound cannot be healed. Frida is weeping because there is absolutely nothing that can be done, because this is her fate.

Strange, though, that hardly a drop of blood trickles from the wounds left by the hammered nails, as if her body had long since been dead.

Her canvases were small so that they could fit on her lap-easel or on the slightly bigger easel in the studio. She painted only a few large canvases. The Maestro, on the other hand, painted huge surfaces, entire halls, walls ten meters high. His frescoes buzzed with people and ideas. Though she truly admired him, she was never tempted to imitate him. For the Maestro, however, ideas were more important than people, and that, she noticed, sometimes translated into ideology. And where he led, she followed. He had the force of personality to draw people to him and to his ideas—but only in life, not in art. Her paintings were too small for the oppressed masses, for the workers and their class struggle. Where would she fit all the rebelling masses and all the Aztecs, Toltecs,

Indios, peasants, revolutionary leaders and historical figures who crowded his frescoes? All those banners and industrial machines and people marching in their thousands toward a better future? That required room. The Maestro's large body needed space to give flight to his art; her paintings were more like her: small and sharp, exact and terrifying.

Still, she was a member of the Communist Party of Mexico. She resigned when the Maestro was kicked out but joined again later. She took part in protest marches, sang the Internationale, hated injustice and believed that communism would save the world from poverty. With comrade Stalin in the lead. His unfinished portrait still stood on the easel in the corner. Like a gray blot. Like a mote. Her own communism rarely went beyond lip service, though she did collect money for the Spanish Civil War. Otherwise, it all boiled down to words, songs, banners, speeches and solidarity with the Maestro. And to a few bad pictures, which she preferred to forget. Bad pictures were unforgivable. They were more a reflection of her love for the Maestro than her love for communism. She did not think he was particularly fond of them; he had an incorruptible eye. Nor was she sure how much he believed in her communism.

The easel with its unfinished portrait of Stalin caught her eye. Why had she never painted Leon Trotsky? Was it because of her own feelings for the man or because the Maestro had broken off with him?

At the end of their first year in Mexico, when it was already all over between them, Frida gave Trotsky a self-portrait for his fifty-

eighth birthday. It is softer than her other self-portraits. Wearing a pastel-colored shawl and green-bordered orange skirt, she is standing on what looks like a stage, draped by light curtains of the same color. Her face is carefully made up, her hair neatly arranged, her lips bright red and her cheeks pink—it almost looks like a billboard for a theater show. She is holding a bouquet of flowers as if she had just received them from an adoring fan. There are no dramatic details in the painting, no wounds or blood or animals. It is a gentle, unobtrusive picture, using her charm again, as she did in her first self-portrait for Alex. The painting is a memento.

When she presented him with the canvas, Trotsky kissed her warmly on the cheek. His wife Natalia examined the picture closely. Still suspicious, she looked for any signs of intimacy. She did not find them and was assuaged. But, when they eventually moved out of the house, Trotsky had to leave the portrait behind.

When the passengers disembarked from the *Ruth* in Tampico Harbor that morning, Frida's eyes locked on Trotsky. Not because he was striking-looking, but because she was so excited to meet a real hero of the communist revolution, not to mention one of the Maestro's idols. In her eyes the huge tanker was carrying just one passenger, a small, slightly stooped older man, with glasses and a gray goatee. He was wearing a tweed jacket, plus-fours and a beret on his head. Frida was there to welcome him on behalf of the Maestro and in her capacity as hostess and interpreter. He and his wife Natalia would be staying at her parents' home.

It was only after seeing Trotsky that she turned her attention to his companion. Natalia was like his shadow, walking half a step behind him. At first Natalia was reluctant to disembark. Yet another unknown country, yet more unknown people. How could she be sure that the people welcoming them were really their friends? After a year of being on the run and living in exile, she did not know what awaited them next.

Almost two decades later, Frida thought back to that moment. Natalia, it turned out, had been right to be afraid. If they had not disembarked in Mexico that day, if they had followed Natalia's instinct, maybe Trotsky would still be alive, she reflected.

At the time, however, she had been irritated by Natalia's hesitancy. Despite her elegant coat, high heels and hat, Natalia seemed unnoteworthy. Whether because of the long voyage, the cold or fear, she was quiet and seemed unsure of herself, lost somehow. Frida immediately realized that the woman was used to being treated as her husband's shadow, an anonymous extra on the movie set of his life. Frida's attention was focused on Trotsky. They had barely met and he was already complimenting her on her looks. What a beauty, I've heard so much about you, but now, seeing you in the flesh like this . . . Then he stopped, as if at a loss for words, his eyes sparkling with genuine admiration. Frida laughed and started telling him about the Maestro, the climate, the house. Trotsky was charming and loquacious. As they drove toward the train station, where the official welcome was planned, Frida already felt completely relaxed. Catching her own reflection in Natalia's eyes, she looked to herself like a garish, screeching parrot. And whenever she noticed somebody's disapproval or even mere reserve, she became that much louder, that much more bombastic.

During their first year in Frida's parents' house, Natalia could not but have noticed how much time Trotsky was spending with Frida, how he kept finding more and more excuses for them to be together—excursions, meetings, trips. She could not but have heard the peals of laughter coming from his studio, fragments of their conversation, words that she could not understand but that sounded gentle and tender. Their relationship began with meaningful looks over dinner. Then Trotsky would offer to lend her a book. Later among its pages she would find letters from him with salacious proposals. She liked his boldness and decided to pick up the gauntlet.

Initially it had been Kity who had attracted his eye. He would touch her leg under the table or stop her in passing and invite her into his room. He was interested only in sex, not in romance, Kity decided. Anyway, she was not all that impressed by him and, unlike her sister, did not admire him enough to succumb.

When they became lovers, both Frida and Trotsky tried to maintain the appearance of a friendly but formal relationship. She was twenty-nine years old and flattered by the attentions of this world-famous revolutionary, this brilliant intellectual. She admired him the same way she did the Maestro. Maybe what attracted her most to Trotsky was the simple fact that the Maestro admired him. Along with a subconscious desire to take her revenge because of the Maestro's affair with Kity.

They would meet in Kity's apartment. The bodyguards,

secretary, maids, driver, Kity, they all knew about the relationship. Even Natalia knew. Everybody knew except for the
Maestro, who seemed to be blind to it all, ignoring even the
most obvious signs.

Every day Trotsky would dictate his biography of Lenin
to his secretary Jean. When Frida entered his study, he would
send Jean off to make tea. Once, when leaving the room and
buttoning up her blouse, she ran into Natalia. They both
stopped in their tracks, the one with her pale face framed by
gray hair and the other with her burnished complexion, loose
hair and bare shoulders. Natalia's quiet sadness frightened
Frida. There was something about Natalia that reminded her
of herself. She recognized the despair of a woman betrayed.
She reached out as if to touch, maybe even embrace her. She
felt the need to comfort her, to tell her that it was nothing
serious on her part, that Natalia had no need to worry. If only
she had been able to, she might even have told her that she
was doing this because of the Maestro. I want to hurt him the
same way he hurt me when he was with Kity, she would have
said.

But Natalia did not speak English and Frida could not
communicate with her. Already weakened by malaria and
fears for her younger son, who was interned in a labor camp
in the Soviet Union, Natalia withdrew into the house, even
wearier, even more worried. She was fifty-five years old, and
had spent the last thirty-five with Trotsky. She knew he was a
skirt-chaser; she had learned to live with it. But Leon's desire
for Frida left her utterly devastated and helpless. She could
do nothing to stop it. Silently she watched his displays of ten-

derness, waiting for him to notice that she too existed, that she too had feelings. And that he was all she had. Patience was her only weapon, patience and the belief that, if she waited long enough, her husband would come back to her.

Natalia turned away and walked down the corridor. For a second, Frida's hand remained suspended in midair.

The Maestro behaved as if he hadn't noticed a thing. She wondered whether he might not even be flattered by the attention his wife was receiving from his revolutionary idol. Toward the end, when she lost interest in Trotsky, she realized that her revenge had completely missed its mark and that all she had achieved was to feel like a pawn.

Because neither man's life revolved around women. The Maestro lived for his art. Trotsky for the revolution. Women, even much-loved women, did not occupy a central place in their lives. Love affairs were a by-product, something that was their due, that went with success and with fame, whether it was in art or in the revolution. Natalia understood this and she knew that all she could do was wait. Her husband would sometimes succumb to a kind of fever, like an infection. The symptoms were always the same and she knew them by heart: restlessness, the shivers, effusiveness, lust, maybe even insomnia . . . The only cure was to possess the woman he was chasing. Then the fever would pass relatively quickly and Natalia could heal the aftereffects, which were usually short-lived and not very dramatic. She could have told Frida all that if she had known how. And she could have quoted to her by heart the letter that he would write to Natalia once Frida left him:

I love you so much, Nata, my one and only love, my true love, my victim . . .

Frida still remembered how during that first period of infatuation and fascination with Trotsky, she had been put off by the passive old woman and despised her for lurking and waiting in the shadows. But she was ignorant of the Natalia who had been educated at the Sorbonne, had studied the history of art, been a revolutionary in her own right and later had become not just his common-law wife (who needed bourgeois conventions like marriage?) and the mother of his two grown sons, but also his secretary and companion in exile. About this Natalia, Frida knew nothing.

Lying in bed early that morning, she thought about Natalia. From her she had learned that it is only if you yourself have been persecuted and threatened that you can really appreciate what it means to be together with your man. And how you don't realize it until somebody else becomes his only refuge, his only home.

One day the two women found themselves alone together in the kitchen and Frida offered Natalia a cup of tea. After a moment's hesitation, Natalia joined her at the table. It was pouring cats and dogs outside and they listened to the soothing, monotonous drum of the rain. At one moment, for want of words, Natalia opened the bag she had been clutching with both hands as if afraid that somebody would steal it from her, and pulled out two photographs. She held them out to her over the table, over the golden liquid in the two porcelain Chinese teacups, over the teapot with its painted hunting scene, and over the cake dish. The photographs were small, their edges serrated. One was of her younger son—Sergei 1911, it said on the back. He was holding a toy, a little dog or teddy bear, maybe. The other son, named Leon after his father, had the serious face of an older brother. They were dressed in sailor suits. These were not formal pictures taken in a studio. Somebody, their father, maybe, or a friend, had called the breathless children over from their game of ball in the garden and told them to stand in front of the camera. Leon and Sergei were still sweaty, they were thirsty and eager to go back and play. Natalia never stopped worrying about them, she knew only too well that she could not protect them from the fact that Trotsky was their father. Frida had learned from Trotsky that Sergei was in the Krasnoyarsk labor camp; they did not know if he was still alive. Leon, Jr., lived in Paris. Although they were grown men now, the pictures Natalia had taken out of her purse immortalized them as boys.

She also knew about Trotsky's two daughters from his first marriage. Zina had committed suicide in Berlin in 1933. Nina had died earlier from tuberculosis. But until that moment when she saw the white-edged photographs of the boys' tiny faces, Frida hadn't realized that these pictures were all Natalia had left of their life together. Yet Natalia displayed no emotion, as if none of this had anything to do with her anymore, as if it all belonged to some distant past. She had taken the pictures out only because she thought it might help Frida understand how their life had been destroyed. *Stalin*, Natalia said, looking out the window, into the courtyard. As if this single name explained everything.

Frida held the photographs, not knowing what to do with them. She wondered if she should put them on the table or give them back to Natalia. And what she should say or do. When she finally reached out and touched her hand she found that the skin was dry and warm.

Suddenly a different Natalia was sitting in front of her, a woman who had shared her deepest fears with her. This woman, who, fleeing Stalin's wrath, had gone from Alma-Ata and Oslo, Turkey and France and now had come to them in Mexico, moved her. This woman who did not know what the next stop on her journey would be. The only proof she had of her former life were the photographs of her two sons.

Even if she had known Russian, Frida could not have defended Stalin. Not in front of this woman.

Her eyes strayed to Stalin's portrait at the back of the room. She knew that this, her last painting, would remain unfinished. She had long been too weak to finish it. Whenever she picked up her paintbrush, she would remember that afternoon and Natalia, the rain drumming on the roof and the children's faces in the photographs. Not long after their tea, Leon, Jr., was killed in a hospital in Paris. Sergei disappeared, vanished, also probably murdered.

Why did I ever want to paint his portrait? she wondered, making out Stalin's face on the canvas in the dawn light. For the same reason that she had gone on the protest march with the Maestro the other day, in spite of the rain, the cold and herself. To be with him, to show him that she would always be with him. This portrait of Stalin had simply been another way for her to get closer to the Maestro: look, I'm with you,

I understand you. It was one of Frida's (Natalia's, a woman's) strategies—to hold on to your man by supporting what is important to him, in this case his politics and ideology. She did everything she could. She joined the Communist Party, then resigned when he was expelled, only to join again later, toward the end, when it was all she had left. She even stopped seeing Trotsky and Natalia after the Maestro fell out with them politically. She learned his rhetoric. She learned how to talk about things that mattered to him, about the revolution, poverty, rights, the working class. She believed in the same ideas. She was never entirely successful, though; she knew that she wasn't completely convincing and that her paintings belied her words. They showed that what she really cared about was not ideology but her own pain, they showed that her art was not in the service of the revolution. Every time she tried otherwise, the results were poor. The Maestro respected her art too much not to realize what was at issue. He never told her what to paint or how.

Natalia returned the photographs to her purse and took out another. It was a picture of the young Trotsky, thick dark hair spilling over his brow, a smile on his face, relaxed. It had obviously been taken long before all his children had been killed and before his own life had turned to one of flight. *He is my "dusha," the soul of my soul*, Natalia said, placing her hand on her breast. Frida had an instinctive dislike of such pathos. Natalia was wearing a dark blue dress and her pale liver-spotted hand stood out against the dark fabric. Frida's throat went dry. She felt the sadness with which Natalia lived her life now.

She did not need to know Russian to understand. But she did know the word *dusha*, she had learned it from Natalia's husband. *Dusha, my soul*, he would say to Frida, kissing her face, her neck, her breasts. Trotsky's ultimate betrayal, she thought at the time, was that he had spoken that same word to both Natalia and her.

She remembered the simplicity of her gestures and words. No one had ever described what she herself felt for the Maestro quite like Natalia. Because that was what the Maestro was—the soul of her soul, the center of her universe, life itself. Many years later she painted *Diego and I*. Thinking of Natalia, she painted tears in her eyes. It was not until decades later that she understood this woman who had been sapped of all strength and color, this woman who existed solely through her husband. Looking after him was the only thing that still kept her alive. She provided a refuge for his restless, driven soul. She was like a second skin to him.

What if the prerequisite for ideal love is that the soul of the one can move into the empty void of the other? she wondered after that encounter. She was not that sure she knew the answer.

Two years later, in August 1940, Natalia's fears for Trotsky proved right. A man whom Frida knew, and whose girlfriend worked for Trotsky, murdered him with an ice pick.

When she heard the news, she immediately imagined Natalia entering his study and finding him in a pool of blood on the floor, the ice pick lodged in his skull. She must have felt his soul fly out of her breast, leaving behind icy desolation.

You're like a comet streaking across the night sky, Trotsky once told her. She liked the metaphor. A ball of fire that scorches everything it touches until it burns itself out. Where do those colors of yours, that joy of life, that *alegría* come from? he wanted to know. From having death close by, she replied. His piercing blue eyes looked at her from behind his lenses. And all I've got left to defend myself is self-discipline, he muttered, more to himself than to her.

Like her, Trotsky was a fighter, and she liked the fact that they had this trait in common. He was never defeated by difficulties. He lived as if in defiance of the circumstances, of fate, the gods, tyrants. She was sad when she heard of his death. They had not seen each other for more than two years because he had fallen out with the Maestro, whom he had accused of being a Stalinist. She remembered how this man, this "old man," as she used to call him, though he was only eight years older than the Maestro, had behaved like a youngster in her presence, temporarily forgetting about Natalia, his dead children, his life on the run. And how grateful he had been to her for giving him these moments of oblivion.

But when she learned the details, she was appalled and thought that there was something almost inhuman about his brutal death. She heard that he would not let the guards finish off the assassin, Mercader. He was still conscious enough to stop them. Don't kill him, he's got to talk, he said, lying on the floor in a pool of his own blood. She knew Trotsky well enough to realize that this was not about pity for another human being whose fate he held in his hands, but about the place Trotsky would occupy in the annals of history. As he lay dying, Leon Trotsky wanted this man, his killer whose alias was Ramón Mercader, to go on trial and confirm that Stalin had ordered the assassination. He knew that the assassin's life was important to his own, Trotsky's, immortality. She was fascinated that he managed to maintain such an iron will even as he was drawing his last breath. He, not Stalin, was made of iron, she thought at the time.

She could not take her eyes off of Stalin's portrait. It was too late for her to destroy this testimony to her own fragility and despair. She thought how she must have been out of her mind when, a year earlier, she had called his death a loss. She could allow herself some self-irony now, but that was how she had experienced his death at the time. She had spent the last year in a kind of religious fervor. It was due to her physical condition, her already manifest decline. And when you are falling apart, you have to find something to hold on to, something that will keep you going. She returned to politics, because politics, like love, created a bond. It was a means of communication, it could help her live a little longer. Stalin had epitomized the struggle against fascism. She was not the only one to turn a blind eye to the labor camps of Siberia or the assassination of Trotsky and his sons. The European left, even her own friends and the Maestro, had suffered from the same form of blindness.

As with every religion, so with communism, belief in the idea was more important than the crimes committed in its name, she thought, watching the light in the room grow stronger.

She again remembered the two little photographs of Natalia's dead sons. Natalia was sitting devastated and soulless somewhere in Mexico City when Frida, eight years after Trotsky's assassination, rejoined the Communist Party, saying that she wanted to dedicate her life to the revolution and paint *something useful*. Can a person change that much? she wondered, though she knew the answer was yes. It was the pills that had done this to her. And the alcohol. And the drugs. And the pain, whose demon had spun out of control.

It's useless for me to be ashamed of those paintings now, she thought. After her various back operations four years earlier, she could feel herself sliding toward the abyss. The amputation had been the last stop on that road. She was less and less sure of her hands. First she lost control of the colors. They became murky, as if they each had too much gray in them. She painted with dirty brushes and in sweeping strokes, layer upon layer. The erosion of her art became increasingly visible, from how she mixed her colors to her choice of motif. And it was progressive, like the gangrene. Like the infection that moved from her leg, through her blood, onto her canvases. Painting requires precision and control and she had lost both. She told herself that the paintings were devoted to the revolution, but she knew they were simply bad paintings. Clumsy, chaotic, stupid pictures. Because the disease had now spread to her mind. Communism had been her last connection with the world and she was distraught that her hand could not follow her ideals. As if her body knew that joining the revolution meant her total defeat, the end.

The coats of paint on the canvas and makeup on her face became thicker and thicker.

She was disappearing, she could feel it in her fingertips.

The little girl in her had never removed the death mask.

After her toes were amputated, she thought more and more about suicide. She told the Maestro that she couldn't paint anymore. When you're holding the brush and your hand trembles, she told him, when you can't mix colors anymore, when your vision becomes blurred, when you lose control and feel the irresistible pull of fatigue, then you have to give up. It's not just that I can't control my hand anymore, I can't even think. I have nothing to say anymore and I know it'll get worse, not better. What would you do? she asked him. Stay with me, stay for my sake, I need you, the Maestro replied, not answering her question.

At the time, it sufficed to believe that he needed her. That was enough to feed her vanity. But now she thought that he hadn't really understood her question. The Maestro had never known that kind of agonizing helplessness, that feeling of losing control.

Forgive me, if you can, Natalia, for Stalin's portrait. I painted it because of the Maestro. Yes, it was my excuse for so many of the stupid mistakes I made. I thought that if I sacrificed my need to express pain in my art, he would pay attention to me again. But what kind of a sacrifice is it when nobody needs or asks for it, and when ultimately you get nothing out of it? It was ridiculous to think that if I painted pictures "useful" to the revolution it might strengthen my relationship with the Maestro. It was a cheap idea and trade-off. He never asked me to paint politically engaged pictures; he knew only too well that my last paintings, including the portrait of Stalin, were acts of despair.

When you start falling apart the way I did, what have you got left? I believed in myself, in my strength to overcome this illness. I no longer have that strength. I believed in my own self-invented myth of love. Even that is no longer enough to keep me going. Because after a while, my possessive love of the Maestro became a lethal poison for us both. And the poison is killing me. But first I have to confess that I betrayed not only you but myself as well. These last few years I've turned more and more into a sick, ragged madwoman sinking her claws into the living flesh of her victim, living off of its warm blood. For a long time I was the Maestro's victim, but now he has become mine.

The only way I exist now, Natalia, is by feeding off the lives of others, like a parasite.

You are a civilized person and at least knew how to discreetly suppress your own personality, how to live in the shadow of a genius. You devoted yourself to him and it worked. I envied you your ability to destroy yourself in order to make room for somebody else, and at the same time I despised your slavish behavior.

My own reckless nature always made me wrap myself around a man like ivy until I started to choke him. I've felt for a long time that I'm a burden to him and that both of us have become losers. I'm afraid I've turned into a man-eating plant. I'm afraid for myself. I know that if I really care about the Maestro I'll have to remove myself from his life as soon as possible.

Nobody can share my suffering, not even the Maestro. He knows how much I suffer, but to know is not the same as to suffer with me, she thought.

In her paintings she spoke the language of pain. But once the painting was completed, it was no longer just her pain, no longer just her experience that she was expressing. Anybody could identify with her and feel her pain as *his own*. However dramatic they were, her paintings elicited not only empathy but also immediate identification with one's own suffering. Once completed, the paintings no longer belonged to her. They outgrew her. When the Maestro looked at her paintings, he saw his own pain as well. She knew that; it marked both her triumph and her defeat.

In the spring of 1938, André Breton was visiting Trotsky in Mexico and met Frida. He admired her paintings, calling them surrealist. She laughed, shaking her head. No, she said, they're simply autobiographical. I paint my life, nothing more. I paint my pain. He did not understand that her life was surrealism personified. His favorite painting was *What Water Gave Me*. He saw the exotic in it, imagination, dreams . . . She saw her own memories. He proposed that Frida participate in an exhibition in Paris in March 1939. The Maestro persuaded her to do it and she saw it as an obligation. The show Breton had mounted was amateurish and superficial, she wrote home later.

She was cold in Paris that spring (she was cold everywhere except in Mexico). She stayed with the Bretons in their shabby apartment, where she shared a bedroom with their daughter. She ended up in the hospital with a kidney and bladder infection. Had it not been for Breton's wife Jacqueline, with whom Frida had made friends and who had scoured the markets with her in search of old dolls, for her collection, Frida would have been utterly lost. When she left Paris she took with her only two old dolls, and unhappy memories.

At the opening of the show "Mexique" at the Pierre Colli Gallery, she felt as if she herself were on display, like an element of Mexican folklore. Miró, Kandinski, Duchamp were all captivated by her paintings. The critics raved, but she was angry with Breton because he had put her paintings alongside photographs, pre-Columbian sculptures and his own collection of the kind of kitsch that was sold on the Day of the Dead: skulls made of sugar, paper skeletons, dolls, flowers, sweets . . . The cover of *Vogue* carried a photograph of her ringed hand, dubbing it the "Madame Rivera" look. She was well on her way to becoming a surrealist icon, but she was not interested. Picasso was enchanted and gave her tortoiseshell earrings of two miniature hands which quickly became her favorite pieces of jewelry. And he taught her a Spanish song about a little orphan, which she often later hummed.

She did not believe that she was famous even when the Louvre bought one of her self-portraits. She was not vain as a painter. As with anybody suffering from a serious illness, for her the fact that she was alive was reward enough. Sometimes she would stop in the middle of cooking, the sauce dripping from the wooden spoon in her hand, or she would be holding a bread knife and stare at the bread crumbs or knife marks on the cutting board. Or she would catch sight of the paint on the tip of her brush before it touched the canvas, the taste of food still in her mouth. She would stand there, suddenly acutely aware of every item, of her every movement and breath, of being present in her body, in the world. The certainty of her existence, if only briefly, that day, that moment, in that place, would be undeniable, vivid.

Such moments gave her life a different meaning. Whatever happened beyond the mere act of survival was, as far as she was concerned, a plus. If survival was success in itself, then everything else became relative.

Depicting herself as an exotic, charming amateur, downplaying the importance of art in her life so as to avoid exposure to serious judgment and competition, was not just because of her relationship with the Maestro. Even when critical acclaim was hers in Paris and New York, Frida remained somehow untouched by it. She enjoyed being the center of attention and having her paintings sold, but that was all.

Her paintings were *small and unimportant*, as she was wont to say, not in comparison with the Maestro's, but in comparison with her fundamental experience of being. And this awareness had a liberating effect on Frida.

That was why she could paint her own abortion, her broken back, her bleeding heart and unhealed wounds from her operations. When you look at Tree of Hope, *it is easy to imagine the surgeon's scalpel gliding down the back of the woman on the bed, slicing open her tender skin. Then he cuts deeper, opening the flesh until the scalpel reaches the bone and the vertebrae. The painting is so suggestive it makes you shudder. But even the two eye-catching, bloody incisions are not as surprising as the corset that the other Frida, who is sitting next to the still-unconscious one, is holding in her hand. The corset is pink, it looks decorative—not like an "instrument of torture," as Frida used to call it—and is like the one worn under her wide red skirt.*

The corset confined her movements, was uncomfortable and painful, but it held her back straight and allowed her to move and to sit and paint. It took not only a certain detachment but also a sense of humor to paint the corset the color of a spring frock, the color of hair ribbons and icing on a child's birthday cake; to even strive for the delicate hue of an oleander blossom and imbue this somber painting with airy cheerfulness.

There is one element here, however, that is easy to overlook. What enables Frida to paint is not only the corset but her own iron will. In order to paint at all she first has to put on that very same pink corset; only then can she sit down in front of the canvas, or pull herself up into a sitting position in bed. Before getting dressed (if she feels well enough that day, she may not need any help in that department), she first has to put on the corset. And she had had a wide variety of them, from plaster contraptions that immobilized her and sometimes kept her bedridden for long periods of time, to more or less flexible leather, plastic or metal constructions like the one held in her hand. Once the corset was on, she could don the wide skirts that hid it. It did not suffice for her to be self-disciplined, like other painters; Frida also had to be able to bear the discomfort of wearing the corset.

She would sit and paint until fatigue set in and the pain became unbearable. Sometimes it would be for only twenty minutes or so. It was a daily battle and depended on the kind of pain she developed from sitting in the same position that long. It could be a momentary, piercing pain that would pass if she changed position, or it could be a dull, milder pain signaling the permanent presence of an inflammation. A fever often accompanied the pain and then she would feel as if her bones were breaking and her body was being crushed to pieces. With that kind of pain, which was exhausting and unrelenting, she would quickly put down her brush and stop painting. Sometimes she thought the piercing pain was easier to bear because, even if it took her breath away, it gave her moments of respite. Usually, though, she was on the uncomfortable edge of pain, which, with the help of Demerol injections, she was almost able to ignore, even forget, as she focused on her painting.

When she contracted pneumonia she refused to go to the hospital. It would have made it easier on everybody if she had agreed to go, but she was pigheaded and said no. Anyway, everybody thought she would recover, because pneumonia was nothing terrible, she had survived worse. What neither Kity nor the Maestro realized was that she had had enough of *surviving*, period. Her body had run its course of illness, scars, pain and weariness. And the body remembered. It slowly counted until it reached the sum total. The difference between Frida and them was that she was aware of it. Clothed in her prettiest dresses, clinging to her skeleton like a faithful partner, she readily danced the tango of death.

And yet, had there been no accident there would have been no painting. Or life with the Maestro. She would have been a country doctor—she had wanted to study medicine. She would have been somebody else. The experience of pain and all those operations was the connecting thread between her life and her art, tying them together like a surgeon sewing up a wound. They were like an umbilical cord, the paintings nourished by her placenta, sucking in her life.

But now her dance had come to an end. Not just because of the pneumonia, which this time did not go away; she could see it on the faces of the people around her. Kity usually entered the room very quietly, in case Frida was asleep. And she was right, of course, because Frida was either asleep or, thanks to the pills and medicine, in that pleasant limbo between sleep and consciousness. But these last few days she had sensed that Kity, for all her efforts, was behaving differently. She was not as thoughtful as before. As if she's practicing how to live once I'm gone, she thought. That's something you have to get used to if you want to go on living yourself. It was nothing obvious, an inadvertent noise would give her away, the moving of a chair, for instance. Or the coldness that now inhabited her eyes when she looked at the bed as if it were already empty.

Kity sensed that this was the end. She knew that the dying could not take much longer. There was little of Frida left in that disintegrating body. She was departing. Every day she spent more and more time in that state of limbo. There she felt no pain, but she did not feel herself either.

For some time she had been unable to pinpoint the source of the pain that had long since become a part of, almost a synonym for, her body, but now it had become all-invasive. Now she had not a moment of peace; the pain was constant.

Disintegration is the only word that comes to mind. How stupid of me to have harbored any hopes. For what? For the pain, my demonic lord and master, to vanish forever? For the intervals between the pain to get longer, not shorter? What was the point of all that self-delusion? Maybe it was to stop me from completely losing my mind. I suppose when it all became too much, it seemed smart to hope. Actually, I behaved very rationally. I had my tactic. My body governed my entire life. I hated being reduced to that dreadful instinct of self-survival, to that point where you say to yourself, Whatever the cost, it doesn't matter, just let me live! Lame, lopsided, broken, half dead. And by now dead, stone cold. How many days or hours have I got left? Something inside me is still holding on to this pathetic wreck of a body, but the rot is spreading and about to consume me.

Worst of all, I know that even this remnant of the remnant of my body would find the strength to go on. Without a leg, without both if need be, without an arm. There is so much you can live without. But maybe not without heart? The body would go on, it would. But can that be called living? Worst of all, the body has even accepted life devoid of pleasure. Because we're not one and the same anymore. The fact that I still feel my body, that, see, I can move, turn onto my side, cough, stretch, doesn't mean a thing anymore. It makes me sick. This broken wreck disgusts me, I can't stand this subtenancy anymore. And here I am, in the end, defeated. Because what am I doing? With the little sanity I've got left I'm trying to see what remains of my individual parts and counting the number of operations I've had.

Why not count the number of orgasms I've had? There were certainly more than thirty-two. But I forgot them a long time ago; pleasure is forgotten sooner than pain.

I can tell from the smell that this is the end. I can already hear the earth shamelessly shifting to make room for me.

In the painting Roots, *fleshy green plants are already sprouting out of Frida's body. They coil around her frame like the tentacles of an animal, crawling out, penetrating deeper and deeper into the cracks of the dry soil. Thin, veinlike little roots spurt from their tips, full of blood. It is only a matter of time before all of her blood seeps into the thirsty soil. Her heart has already been bled dry, so has her womb; you can see a part of the landscape through the hole that is in its place. The body is still whole, though. Maybe she hadn't had the strength to paint the decomposition of living flesh, and so at first you might think that this is yet another one of her decorative if morbid paintings, with its excess of beauty. Did she use beauty to arouse pity for the woman/herself lying there, being quietly devoured by the plants? But a closer look at the painting shows Frida resting her elbows on a pillow, as if sunbathing rather than half vegetable herself. The self-irony precludes pity and causes confusion.*

Her eyes are open, she is still alive even though she is already sprouting man-eating plants. The beauty of the living corpse is hardly flattering or easy on the eye. On the contrary. The well-shaped body is here to underscore its inexorable dissolution into plant food, into fertilizer. Which is why the dying Frida arouses not pity but horror in the face of death, whose seed we all carry in our belly. The gigantic plant that has germinated from that seed is tearing her belly apart before its time.

But why is she so serene, then, why is she showing no signs of agony? Because she has been in agony for too long and has become used to it. She is someone who suppresses pain and despises death. She is lying on the ground, a minor concession so that the viewer can appreciate the closeness of death. If she were laid out on a bed, all those leaves might seem like mere decoration rather than the ivy of death that they are, deliberately coiling around everything except her neck, refusing to cut short her misery. Her excruciating pain becomes obvious, her scream comes not from her open mouth but from the very sight of her body being devoured by plants. How can people understand her suffering unless this painting jolts them into experiencing it for themselves?

Yesterday, though she was no longer sure if it was yesterday or some other day, Kity brought her some fresh roses. Those dark red ones aptly called Don Juan. She had buried her face in the bouquet, inhaling its fragrance. I'm so tired, she had said. Kity understood, she knew exactly what she meant. She had recently been giving her the painkilling injections. She knew where Frida hid her stashes of Demerol and morphine. It was simple. A bit more of the blissful substance in the syringe and she would never wake up.

Set me free from this terrible prison, she said. She realized that she was now begging Kity for release just as she had once begged her for love.

But Kity did not reply. She said neither yes nor no. Lifting Frida's head, she placed a glass of water against her dry lips. Then she put a fresh compress of diluted vinegar on her forehead. She placed her own cool hand on Frida's burning one and kept it there until the temperature started to drop. Frida's breathing was shallow, every breath she took was an effort. Please, she implored softly. *Please*.

Before she left, Kity placed the roses in a vase and put the vase on the table so that Frida could see them. I'll come back tomorrow afternoon, she said. Tomorrow afternoon, Frida thought, her tomorrow is so far away.

She felt as if she were on fire. Pricks of light danced before her eyes and she could not recognize objects in the room even though the light was stronger now. How much longer would she have to wait for the end?

And why wait at all?

For a long time now, death had taken the Maestro's place in her bed. They had a tacit agreement that even though she could feel its presence, Frida would ignore it. It was a silent partner, it had no need to assert itself. Death would leave her alone until her time came. And now that time had come.

The Maestro cannot bear to see you like this, Kity had said the other day. He loves you too much to watch you suffer. He's a coward, she replied, regretting the words as soon as she had said them. Poor man, it was not his fault that he could not watch disintegration and death, she thought. He usually came early to kiss her good morning. How are you, my love?

he would ask, not knowing what else to say. And what could she give as an answer? I'm fine, she would say, fine, I'm better today. She would be lying, of course, but it was easier for both of them that way. She was tired of telling the truth because it didn't lead anywhere anymore. She was not going to get better, that was certain, so why waste words? It was not so long ago that she was giving him detailed daily reports, enumerating exactly what hurt, how, and where. She was tired of it, so why wouldn't he be? Anyway, he couldn't help her anymore. All she could do was make him feel guilty that he was of no use, and even that feeling would quickly revert to self-pity. It was all so predictable. She knew that her answering "I'm fine," would give him a clear conscience, her blessing for him to proceed with his life as if everything were all right.

You keep telling me you're feeling better, the Maestro said, in teasing rebuke.

It makes no difference what I tell you, my darling, Frida thought. You should know by now that it's what I don't tell you that matters. In my situation, words don't mean a thing. Sometimes I wonder what on earth you see in me, and of me, now . . .

I'd rather you didn't ask, I'd rather not talk. I'd rather you come and lie down beside me and hold me in your arms. And warm me. I'm cold, that's what I'd like to tell you. I can feel the chill of the grave blowing my way. Stay with me until I die, it'll be easier for me if you hold me in your arms, I don't want to die alone. Hold me. It won't take long, I promise. I still have just enough strength to look around and into my heart. Even that is coming to an end now. My hands are cold, my darling, make them warm. I'll leave quietly, look, see how quiet I am. I'm not angry anymore. I'm just waiting now. I've already let even you go, my love, my child. Last night, when I gave you the ring you were not supposed to receive until next week, for our twenty-fifth wedding anniversary, you were so surprised! Why are you giving me the ring now, it's too early, isn't it? you asked. I was happy to see you surprised. You still had hope, I thought, hope, alternating with despair.

I know, my darling, it's hard when you can't help the person you love. When you have to watch her suffer. I'm leaving you, I'll soon be gone, I told you last night. And see, now it's happening. And you're not here. It's too late, it's pointless for me to wonder if you were ever with me in my darkest hours. When I had my first abortion, or when I had my leg and back operations, when they put me in a new corset and when I writhed in agony at night. Because there were always maids and nurses, my sisters and friends around. In my worst moments I had only women by my side, I would not have survived without them. They made me soup, washed me and dressed me. They brushed my hair to make me look beautiful—for you. So that I could keep pretending that I was fine and that this was only a minor setback. It'll go away, I said, it's already going away. I was speaking out of fear, of course. I didn't want to be too heavy a burden to you, to scare you with obligations and responsibilities, to make you tired of all my illnesses. And I was right to be afraid, because you did tire of them, in spite of all my precautions, deceptions and self-delusions. You had neither the time nor the patience to cope with me then, just as you haven't now. You're my beloved, one of those men who never thinks to ask if I need a glass of water. You bring me flowers, but not water. You pay other people, women usually, to take care of me. Yes, I sometimes made scenes and threw things at you. Out of anger, yes, but really because I felt helpless. Because you weren't here when I needed you. But it was no use. You're drawing attention to yourself again, you're not the center of the universe, you know, was your comment. Humiliated, dispirited, all I could do was revert to my role of heroine. The heroine who suffers in silence, who never complains and never makes demands. She does everything alone. Including dying, needless to say.

You usually return in the evening to kiss me good night, though it has been a long time since my nights were good, or my days, for that matter. Something viscid and heavy is enveloping me, layers of it are building up like tar. Is the earth going to be as heavy as this? Every so often, with my last ounces of strength, I surface from this sludge. This struggling and kicking is so typical of me! It is not easy to surrender to death, even when you want to. And sometimes I don't see you for days. You're like a boy playing hooky from school because he hasn't done his homework. Oh, human beings know how to protect and spare themselves, they do! Because somebody else's pain is not your pain. Only your own pain hurts you, it's the only pain that counts. And what does my beloved do? He's already got another woman in reserve. Ema, to make it all the more paradoxical, is comforting you because of me.

I know, you are suffering, but you started consoling yourself a bit early, don't you think? (See, I haven't lost my sense of humor!) I find your behavior funny now, funny and pathetic and unimportant. On the other hand, it shows me how alive you still are, unlike me. I understand, with Ema's help you're saving your own life, you're sparing yourself from future loss and pain. It's all so simple, so transparent. So typically *male*.

I should be nicer to you. Your very presence in my life gave me the confirmation I was looking for, that, in spite of everything, you wouldn't leave me. I got as much as I could from you. But why didn't I ever tell you that, my love? Because I wanted to spare you? Even now? Maybe I'm not sure you would understand me and I don't want to find out. It's better this way. It's myself I'm sparing.

I'm dying. Dying. I know, because I've painted it, that it is a lonely affair. But I can't help wishing you were beside me. Because the hardest thing for me is to part from you. You've been with me all this time, after all. You're the only one who managed to penetrate my loneliness and stay there. I should have told you that too, but I was a coward.

Seriously, my darling Maestro, it was important for me to know that you saw something in my paintings, that they affected you.

She was alone that morning, and afraid. She was neither heroine nor actress anymore. She had been afraid to fall asleep the night before because she did not know if she would wake up. In the morning she was afraid of the day because it lasted too long and only brought her more pain.

She had once read that there is always somebody somewhere suffering some kind of loss. She took the fact that she had survived polio, the accident and even rape by a metal rod as a plus. And she was grateful that, sick as she was, she had lived in a world of healthy normal people. She knew it was stupid to add and subtract losses and gains; such calculations were almost comical and it was an effort for her even to remember.

But she knew that she would cease to exist once she stopped remembering, so she was grateful for this last moment of lucidity.

To be rid of that terrible burden.

To cut the thread.

To relax. To forgive. And to return to nothingness, to nonbeing.

Frida did not care what happened afterward, once she was no more. For her to be her, she needed this body. She had just one last effort to make: to cut this thin connecting thread between consciousness, the body and the outside world. That was the only way she could fly away and finally soar above it all, like that beautiful butterfly that had once alighted on her hand.

She had celebrated her forty-seventh birthday only a week earlier. She knew that it was her last birthday and also her last opportunity to assemble her friends and say good-bye to them. Cristi and Mayet sat her on a chair in the tub, soaped her down and washed her hair.

Frida did not look up. She avoided looking in the mirror opposite the tub. She hung her head, staring at the stump where her leg used to be. Nothing about her body saddened her more than the sight of that rounded stump of pink flesh below the knee. She remembered the smell just before the amputation—the smell came from her own leg. It was the smell of rot, not the choking damp rot of vegetation or the acrid rotting of fruit. Her leg had the stench of leftover meat at the butcher's on a scorching hot day, it reeked of the inhuman, it reeked of death. Maybe she was wrong, but she had the feeling that the smell lingered even after the amputation, even after the wound had healed. It lingered in the corners of the room, the folds of the covers, under the pillows, in her armpits. It would not go away and she wondered if others could smell it too, visitors who would politely say nothing and quickly leave the room. Do you still smell it, Kity? she asked. Or am I hallucinating? Kity tried to comfort her. It's just your imagination, she would say, why, the leg hardly smells at all . . . She would carefully dry and wrap the stump and then help her strap on the shoed artificial limb leaning against the bathroom wall like an excess piece of luggage. It was all the more dreadful because the leg looked so real.

Wearing a white dress and red boots—the symbolic kitsch of the colors did not escape her—she made her entrance. Her staged farewell was, of course, a morbidly cheerful performance. Playing the brave, proud, invincible heroine for the last time, she watched her guests crowd around the table laden with food and tried to look happy. She had worn this mask of happiness all her life. Except in her paintings. Like any clown, she lived a double life. All those years of living with humiliation and loneliness are over now, she thought. People see only what they want to see, only what is front stage center. Understanding somebody means taking responsibility, it means having to help. Even when people wanted to help me I was too proud to let them, she mused, watching her nephew Antonio cram cake into his mouth.

She had not enjoyed herself for a long time. And yet, it was hard for her to say good-bye to all these people, to the house and what was in it. She sat on the chair, looking at the green and meat-red slices of watermelon. They were temptingly juicy. Unlike the dead flesh of her leg. I'm already observing everything from one and the same perspective. It's time for me to go, she thought.

Little Antonio came up to her and sweetly laid his head on her lap. Somebody would be missing her after all. She placed a tired kiss on his soft cheek, carefully, as if afraid she would infect him with her own decay.

The sweet scent of the child's skin. Close. Warm. Skin. The touch of the Maestro's warm skin in bed at night when she would suddenly wake up and clasp his sleeping body, taking in its warmth, inhaling his smell of spice, tobacco and dried fruits. The Maestro smelled so aromatically edible that she could have taken a bite out of his smooth body right there and then, for the pure pleasure of it. Or maybe just to make sure that he really was there beside her. If only she could have remained lying there next to him as he slept.

Sometimes, his mere presence was enough. Breathing quietly, more and more softly.

She was afraid that death would claim her while she was asleep, like in her dream after the accident all those years ago. Sometimes she would wake up choking. Then she would scream. And when no one came she would lie awake trembling until daybreak.

Stroking the boy's head, she thought how hard it was for her to sit with them, pretending she still had some strength left. She was tired of performing.

At eight in the evening, she said good night and retired to her room.

A ray of light fell on the sheet and she wanted to flee from its whiteness. She looked at the syringe on the tray. Another hour, she thought, just one more hour.

She ran her hand over the empty spot on the bed. Her friend Adela had been with her when Dr. Farill had decided that he had to amputate, it would be too dangerous to wait any longer. Frida had slid her leg from under the cover and showed it to her. She had no toes left. Her leg did not look like a part of the human body. She remembered her friend's face when she saw the thing, it looked more like a withered branch than a leg. Removing it was a purely technical matter. It serves no purpose anymore, said the rational Adela, barely concealing her own queasiness. She remembered how she had touched her blackened, deformed leg for the last time. She hadn't felt a thing, not even her skin. She thought, not for the first time, of the fateful role this leg had played in her life. Like the forgotten parasol, like the Maestro climbing down from the scaffold to look at her paintings, like the naked Kity in his studio . . . Or had it all been mere happenstance?

In Natalia's life, the only happenstance had been meeting Trotsky in Paris. Had she not gone to the exhibition that day she would not have met him. Nothing that happened after that was by chance. Natalia's life became ruled by the will and logic of one single man who was persecuting Trotsky. Had Frida not taken a seat in the bus that day she would not have been in the accident, pain would not have inhabited her body and proceeded to rule the rest of her life. Chance is fate, she told herself, touching her already dead leg, bidding it farewell.

Before the operation she had watched a part of her body rot away and imagined the body itself decaying inside a coffin belowground, turning into the same mass of putrid flesh. The idea made her sicker than the actual stench. Promise me you'll have me cremated, she told her sister. Startled, Kity gave her the kind of frightened look that Frida despised and usually found infuriating. Promise me! she shouted. Kity had to promise. And so did the Maestro, though he tried to convince her that she was delirious. What's all this talk about cremation? You'll feel much better after the operation, he said. She knew he was only saying that because she was still capable of raising her voice. She knew his powers of self-deception only too well.

You're so afraid of death, she retorted. The Maestro went pale and, big as he was, leaned over to kiss her in spite of the odor of disease and the stench of her leg. She thought how the Maestro was braver than she was, because she could no longer stand the sweet sickly smell of gangrene. All her life she had hated that sick, disgusting leg, as if it weren't even hers. When they finally sawed it off, the hatred—that dark part of her that she had suppressed all her life and hidden behind a mask of cheerfulness—suddenly surfaced. She was an invalid, and there was no way she could hide it under long skirts or pretend otherwise now. A piece of her body was missing and more than ever she felt exposed and completely unprotected. All her defense mechanisms collapsed. After the operation she hated herself.

As if the disgust she had felt for her leg still remained, poisoning her body.

When she lost her leg, the Maestro ordered a wooden limb. It was perfectly made, shaped like the leg she never had. A firm calf, nicely shaped toes with polished nails, even the color matched that of her own skin. The artificial limb was much nicer than her own, and that made it morbidly attractive. She would pick it up and examine it with a mixture of admiration and curiosity. I'm almost not sorry that I lost my leg now that I have this wonderful replacement, she told Kity, smiling, a month after the amputation. How like her to say something so outrageous, thought Kity. She did not reply. Frida could easily throw that same wooden leg out the window the very next minute. Nobody could keep up with her rapid mood swings.

Along with the artificial limb, she was given a pair of new red boots made of the finest calfskin, with little gold mesh bells. The boots still smelled of fresh leather when she opened the box. She was so happy that for the first time since the operation she smiled at the Maestro, who was standing by her bed, delighted to see her in such a good mood. Don't worry, Frida, you'll be dancing before you know it, he said happily. She hugged her new boots like a child with a new toy. The Maestro had correctly guessed her favorite color and taste. He knew that the boots would remind her of the first pair she had been given as a child after recovering from polio. They had served to conceal her withered leg. She wore them even in the hottest weather until she outgrew them and was given a new pair; she still kept them as a memento of those days. Even with that first pair, she had mastered the art of camouflage. These new red boots would serve to conceal her artificial limb. I'll be able to walk again, even better than with my old sick leg, she said, kissing him in delight.

When she put on her magic boots, as she called them, she felt whole again, if only for a minute. She could fool a passerby. And she was used to fascinating, beguiling, fooling people with her appearance. Walking on a wooden leg was a different story. It required a new kind of strength. She had to learn how to walk again. First she would sit on the edge of her bed and unwrap her stump. Kity would strap on the limb with a leather belt. She had to attach it so that the stump would fit neatly into the cup without chafing her when she walked; the wooden leg had to support her and at the same time feel as comfortable as an old shoe. Then her sister would lift her under her arms and pull her upright onto her feet. She was thin, she weighed less than fifty kilos. You're lighter than a sack of flour, the Maestro would say as he lifted her into her bed. He was amused by the difference in their size—the couple really did look like an elephant and a dove, as their friends used to call them. She seemed so oddly petite and light in the presence of this enormous man. She would just stand there at first, resting on her own leg. She had to find her balance and did not dare to shift her weight onto the other, new leg. After the amputation, the feeling that she still had her own leg was strong, even though it had been replaced by an artificial limb. But she had always been tenacious. Holding on to Kity or the Maestro, on to the bed, the table or a chair, she started taking her first steps.

At first she walked stiffly, as if her body were made of wood. It was only because she wanted to wear her red boots that she persevered. She was irritated by the slow awkwardness of her movements. The doctors assured her that with time her movements would become smoother and she would walk more naturally—as if she had ever been able to do that in the first place.

Her spirits were low, but she kept practicing. The Maestro was thrilled with the progress she was making. Once, when he dropped in unexpectedly and saw her doing something in the kitchen, he knelt down and kissed her wooden leg. It'll all be fine, my love, you'll walk, you'll even dance again, I know you. She stroked his head of thinning gray hair. She was touched by his words but lacked the strength to tell him that it was too late, that she had no energy left to dance.

But dance she did. Later she thought she must have dreamt it, but after only three months of practicing, she was so used to her wooden leg that she really could dance. She twirled with more confidence in her legs than ever before. She was even able to dance the tricky *jarabe tapatío*, whose steps she had learned as a little girl. She would get carried away and forget all about her leg, dancing faster and faster until, breathless, she collapsed on the bed, loving it all. Frida, the one-legged woman, come on over and see her dance! The circus is in town for just one more day, don't miss it, Kity said, laughing. That was the last time that she felt real freedom of movement, even though she had already lost her leg. Her dancing feet echoed on the wooden floor; it was the sound of her victory, yet another victory over her body, and herself. She was on her feet again, she was the old Frida once more.

Boots, orthopedic shoes, corsets, artificial limbs, wheelchairs—all of her life she had needed their support. A withered leg at the start of her life, an amputated leg at the end of it.

And in between those two events—the accident, the Maestro, the effort to survive and conceal her crippled leg, the scars, illness, pain, sadness, loneliness—unbearable loneliness.

The wooden leg momentarily restored her will to live. But learning to walk was pointless when the pain in her back was so bad that she could barely get out of bed. Right after the operation she had felt relief, but she knew that she would never recover, that the osteomyelitis was not going to go away. Walking was not worth the effort anymore. The wheelchair would do for her purposes. She had the pills left, the tranquilizers, sleeping pills, painkilling injections. To quell the pain, to lull the demon, that was all she wanted. She would spill the pills into the palm of her hand and gulp them down. She could not paint anymore. She was conscious of surrendering. She was sinking, disappearing. As if the amputation had been one operation too many.

Her body was giving up, the inner substance of life was

spent. All that was left was the shell, a fragile, translucent carapace like that of a bug.

She felt like a wounded animal dying alone in the woods.

The same seething sky and desolate, arid land as in the painting Girl with Death Mask. *This time the lonely figure is not a child but a deer with a human face. It is a woman's face, Frida's, but she has male antlers on her head. Countless arrows have pierced the deer's body. Blood is streaming from the wounds in the majestic animal's body. At first glance, the deer looks as if it is about to collapse, as any animal that badly wounded would have already done. But not Frida. The animal is painted leaping, it is hard to say whether the wounds, even if profusely bleeding, have penetrated to its heart. Frida's face is calm: you can fire your arrows at me, but they will not kill me. My desire to live is stronger than any wound. The wounds hurt, but I am used to pain. I will survive. Frida the animal will survive. She will not fall to the ground. She will not drag herself off into the woods. Huntsmen and dogs will not catch her. She will escape death, once more.*

The image of the wounded deer kept dancing before her eyes. She knew that the arrows had gone too deep and that it would bleed to death. The deer would fall, it had fallen already. Her new red boots and artificial limb would not help her run from the huntsmen. All she could do was wait for death. Or maybe try to stand up again, just one more time?

Ten days before she died she spent four hours in the rain, demonstrating with the Maestro in support of the Guatemalan government. The doctor had forbidden her to go out.

Predictably, she had disobeyed him. She did not try to walk, she was already too weak for that. She went in a wheelchair. The Maestro pushed the chair and kept asking her if she was cold, checking that she was warmly wrapped up in her blanket. She felt neither hot nor cold. She was with him for those four hours, with people in the street.

In the photograph of her last public appearance, her face is thin and her eyes sunken. She is wearing a scarf over her head and is clearly trying to smile. She looks like a woman of sixty, not someone who is about to turn forty-seven. She strains to raise her right arm and clench her fist. Her pathetically small fist and thin arm are no longer a threat to anyone. The Maestro's hand rests on her shoulder as if to protect her, but to no avail. Nobody could protect Frida from herself.

Thousands of people took part in the march. She listened to the sound of their steps, the sound of human masses. She heard them sing the Internationale, the song started somewhere far up ahead and then reached them in waves. A passerby had dropped a red carnation in her lap and suddenly she thought she was at her own funeral.

Why did she go out and attend the demonstration in the pouring rain, in defiance of her doctor's orders, risking pneumonia? Did she realize the danger? Ideology did not interest her anymore. Nor, since the amputation, did her own health. She simply wanted to be with the Maestro, she wanted to be a part of his life until the very end.

She knew that the end was near when—could it really have been only ten days ago?—she went out to demonstrate without any makeup on, without her hair done or her usual

colorful dress. Normally she would not have allowed herself
to appear like that because she would have felt naked.

Appearance was a declaration of her own existence. It was
not so much a matter of aesthetics as of tactics, of deliberately
calling attention to her imperfections. And even more important, of wanting to feel noticed. She was screaming, Look at
me, I'm alive!

*Her self-embellishment served the same purpose as the frame of
her self-portrait* The Frame, *which is integral to the painting.
The birds and the flowers that enframe her face give the painting
its cheerful, bright quality. The scarlet, pink, orange and blue are
reflected in her face like the sun against the water. The frame actually dominates the painting, though Frida is careful to maintain
a balance so that the eye is not drawn only to the frame and its
suggestion of the exotic. The frame directs the eye to the face. This
is one of her rare self-portraits where there is the trace of a smile.
With a yellow sunflower in her hair against a blue backdrop,* The
Frame, *like all her self-portraits, is an expression of her innermost
feelings.*

Her last carefully executed painting, Self-Portrait with Dr.
Farill, *was also painted without vanity. Frida's hair is neatly
combed but devoid of any embellishments, she is wearing a simple
black skirt and white tunic. Her face looks drawn, her expression
serious. As if it had not been enough for her to paint her wounded
body, she now painted the final stage, her helpless body drooped in a
wheelchair. She denudes herself yet again, but in a new way—how
many ways are there to show the degradation of the body, one won-
ders? The doctor's portrait is meticulous, almost photographic. The*

palette Frida is holding has a huge human heart on it instead of
colors. Blood is dripping from her paintbrush.

But it was not just that she was too weak to do herself up.
She could have asked the maid or Kity or a friend to brush
her hair and braid it with ribbons and flowers. She simply no
longer felt the need. Vanity is connected to the body, to life.
And that day it had already moved on, it had left her.

The mirror was still affixed to the headboard of her bed.
For months she had been observing her transformation into
a caricature of herself. The woman lying in her bed, in her
place, speaking through her mouth, was harder and harder
for her to recognize. When she was made up, her face looked
grotesque. She used black eyeliner, but her hand was not
steady anymore and the lines were spasmodic. She saw two
dark smudges in place of her eyes. And a blood-red hole that
was supposed to be her mouth. The face seemed to be mock-
ing her, saying, You don't live here anymore. Go away, beat
it, once and for all.

She finally took two small bottles of morphine out of the
drawer. Two, just in case. She held them in her hand, to warm
them up.

When she remembered how she had almost died once already, when she recalled all the operations she had had and
the number of times she had painted them—her own and
others', all the skeletons and skulls, her own dead fetuses and
the dead children of others—she wondered what on earth
was keeping her here. What had she still left to do? She had

lived to see the opening of her first Mexican exhibition, celebrated her birthday, seen her friends, bidden farewell in her
heart to everyone, including the Maestro. Those closest to
her knew that her health had been rapidly deteriorating for
the past three years. She had lived on because she had refused
to accept reality. Now she accepted it. She gave up the fight.
Sometimes she would not speak for days on end, just staring
out the window at the courtyard. At the trees, the birds, the
rain. The sky. She was awake but absent. The price of over-
coming the pain was endurance, not life. Because her life was
ruled by Demerol.

And now all she wanted was not to be caught unprepared
when death finally came. Why wait? What right did she have
to beg Kity to give her that lethal injection when she was
still conscious enough to make her own decision, and strong
enough to carry it out? When she was conscious, she was
afraid that she would close her eyes and disappear, unaware
that she was disappearing forever. She didn't know why, but
her fear of dying unawares was greater than her fear of death
itself.

She wished Kity were next to her, holding her hand as she
had done so many times before when they lowered the white
ether-soaked gauze onto her face in the operating theater.

She was calm. The end, she knew, would be no different
from being put to sleep before an operation. It would simply
be a sudden loss of consciousness, nothing dramatic, no tears
or death rattles. She sensed that the only thing still connecting her to this world was her defiant desire not to surrender
to death, for death to be up to her and her alone.

Her thoughts reverted to the suicide of Dorothy Hale. A woman in New York had commissioned Frida to paint the portrait of her friend, the late young actress Dorothy Hale. She presented the macabre picture to the horrified woman, who had wanted to give it to Dorothy's mother as a gift. Instead of a portrait of a lovely girl, Frida had painted her suicide. Like in the movies, she had painted her falling from a skyscraper, first a tiny figure at the top who became bigger and bigger as she fell, until finally she was lying dead on the sidewalk. Stiff as a doll, eyes open, in an elegant black dress without a crease on it. A pool of blood spread out from under her pretty head and her face was flecked with drops of blood. Appalled, the woman later admitted that when she first saw the painting she had wanted to destroy it.

I was so unkind, so hard on poor Dorothy. The painting was so . . . cold. Because I despised suicides. I was mad at her. Because she was young. Because she was pretty. Because she was healthy and because she had thrown it all out the window. It made me sick to think how she had scorned life, had renounced it. If only once she had felt the pain I go through every day, I thought while painting her portrait, if she had had to lie immobile in a plaster cast for just a week, she would not have jumped. She would have rejoiced at every moment that she was without pain and free of the cast. I always thought of suicide as the easy way out and therefore as an act of cowardice. And I couldn't stand cowards. You can always find at least one reason to make you want to take your own life. And it isn't easy to face that void. But it is even harder to live with pain as your resident demon. You have to do the best you can with the cards you've been dealt, because the point of life is living. It's existing, in spite of everything. Feeling, looking, participating. Being happy. We aren't given a second chance or another life.

That's why I was not ready to forgive Dorothy her suicide. And that's why the painting is cold, it doesn't show her loneliness, her suffering or that moment when she found herself on the brink of the abyss, alone. Her serene face doesn't show the horror she must have felt, the scream that rang out that early morning as she plunged through the mist. Or had she maybe, that second before she jumped into the void, been at peace with her decision? Because certainty of any kind does bring a sense of peace.

I discovered later—too late for the painting, though—that there are limits. You have the right to make such a decision when you lose all control over your body and over your life. When you are nothing more than a wreck, a shell, a hull already occupied by death. When life becomes so unbearable that it is not life anymore, it is biological endurance, like being an inanimate object. Except human beings are not inanimate objects. It is then that death comes as a relief.

She had to let go. It was too humiliating to die like this, piece by piece. It was taking too long, she was afraid that people would stop caring. You cannot keep feeling sorry for someone forever, it's tiring, exhausting even. She could see it with the Maestro and Kity, with her nieces and friends, with the doctor, even with the maids. She noticed that their expressions would change once they entered her room, as if they had been standing outside the door, fixing not entirely natural smiles on their faces that barely concealed traces of something else. Impatience? Surprise? Like strands of unwashed hair escaping from under one's cap. True, sometimes happiness showed, they were glad she was still alive—*still* being the operative word. But when the dying is protracted, people have enough of it the moment they know that death is a certainty. After that it is just a matter of waiting. Certainty is not an excuse for impatience—a show of impatience would be rude—no, she could not blame them for their poorly concealed dispassion.

She was departing because that old feeling of helplessness and shame had returned and she had no strength to fight it anymore. Her spirit had been numbed by sedatives, her vision was blurred, her movements heavy and slow. All she could do was cry for help, swear, arouse pity. Worst of all, she had been reduced to the state of a helpless child, except this time there was no hope. Her body was completely spent and withered inside. Yes, she had been sick before, but there had been more to her than just illness. Now death had filled her skin, carrying it around like a coat, adjusting the sleeves, fixing the collar, letting it hang properly, waiting. There was no room left for the person inside. Because death took no interest in the body of the person it occupied. And that person was quickly disappearing anyway. Whatever this disease was called, it was the disease of death.

So suicide was the logical answer. Her decision, she knew,

was one of courage, not weakness or fear. It will be an act of *my own* free will while I've still got it. It will be an act of defiance.

When she reflected on the reasons, she knew that what she needed was tenderness and that the Maestro no longer had time for her, not as much as she needed. How could she tell him that she needed all of his time? She could make him sit by her bedside only if he thought she was really unwell. Then he would sit beside her for an hour or two longer. She knew that by arousing his pity she was doing what she had despised all of her life. She also knew that pity eventually dries up, leaving only a sense of weariness in its wake. The Maestro had found his own way of dealing with her emotional blackmail. She had brought him to the point where he sought escape with his mistress, politics, people—as far away from her sickbed as possible.

After her two abortive suicide attempts in a year, the Maestro kept reassuring her how much he needed her, how he could not live without her. She realized now that he had been lying, that it had been a beautiful, well-meaning lie, but a lie all the same. For her this was only further proof of her own vanity and self-delusion. Because he had been living without her for quite some time already.

She was still moving in her bed, if only a little. Talking, barely. But she was not the same person, and the Maestro knew it. It was only pity and a sense of obligation that brought him to her now. He did not need her anymore, yet another good reason to let go, that and the loss of control, the disintegration.

Forgive me, my darling, I was hard on you. Unnecessarily hard and bitter. I don't want to leave you like that, but I've got no time left for anything except to beg you to forgive me. I was wrong. I expected more of you than you could give. What right did I have? Because I expected more of myself as well? Because I had to ask more of life so that I could get at least something out of it? Simple, probable explanations . . . And yet, it took me a whole lifetime to realize that not everybody is the same and that people do only what they can, give only what they've got—and that it is precious. I was blind, desperately fighting to survive. And I'm afraid that in my shortsightedness I didn't see others as they are but as I thought they should be. I caused the two of us unnecessary suffering. Yes, I see now that I expected more of life than just suffering. Your love, my darling, was supposed to be the answer to all my problems. I saw love as my salvation. Love was my religion. I suppose everybody has a need to imagine their own god. But all it led to was even more suffering and disappointment. Because, of course, there is no salvation.

And in the final analysis, what is love? It seems to me now that it is simply a word for a whole gamut of feelings, from tenderness to solidarity and passion. Because don't forget that, unlike painting or music, language is not a precise instrument. Love is the common denominator, the basket we fill with all sorts of things. Our catchall.

It's too late to tell you now that I placed too big a responsibility on your shoulders, expecting you to make me happy and rescue me in the process. You were my obsession, my fixation. I equated your name with happiness. Of course you couldn't work miracles, because it wasn't in your power. It is my fault, Maestro, that I turned you into a god, gave you the role of a god and then was disappointed when you didn't act like one. What a poor little fool your Frida is, so unbearably demanding, so unbearably unhappy.

And the worst thing is that I was so sure *I had a right* to you, to love, to life. No, there are no rights, no guarantees. You exist, you cope in this life, you're more or less alone and that is it.

You can't give more of yourself than you've got, she thought, remembering an almost long-forgotten incident with a young girl who had killed herself right in front of her. She remembered the dying light in the girl's frantic eyes. She had been obsessed with Frida and dreamt of making love to her. Frida felt nothing but aversion for the girl. Though Frida had forbidden her entry to the house, the maid must have been out that day because the girl suddenely appeared at Frida's studio door.

She started threatening Frida, saying that if Frida did not take pity on her, she would kill herself. Frida burst out laughing. It was a loud, harsh laugh. The crazy girl kept saying that she would kill herself. Frida stood there staring at her. The girl's face was white. Her lower lip was trembling. Frida saw that she was holding a little bottle in her hand, but she didn't move or try to stop the girl from swallowing its contents. She didn't take the girl's threat seriously.

Suddenly the girl gulped down the transparent liquid in

the bottle. Frida watched her collapse as the bottle rolled onto the floor and the girl's skirt hiked up revealing the whitest of thighs. Frida stood there looking down at her but did not move. She did not call for help. She felt nothing as the dying girl stared straight at her.

She had never felt guilty because of what had happened. On the contrary, she had been disgusted by the girl's emotional blackmail and rejection of life. But now for the first time she was disgusted with herself. How was she any different from that girl? Hadn't she been obsessed with the Maestro, hadn't she tried to arouse his pity day in and day out, making him spend time with her against his will? Hadn't she emotionally blackmailed him? And finally, hadn't she herself twice tried to commit suicide in the same way and for the same reason as that crazy girl? The first time, the Maestro had attributed it to a fit of jealousy; the second time, to drunkenness. Both times he had been right, but he never thought about what had triggered these attempts.

Last night, just a few hours ago, actually, she had overheard the doctor warn the Maestro that her condition was rapidly deterioating. Yes, yes, the Maestro had replied absently. But she really is very, very sick, the doctor reiterated. Yes, said the Maestro, proceeding to discuss something else. He had received the information on a par with so much other incidental information he had to process—the bill that he had to pay, his lawyer's letter that he had to answer, the art gallery that he had to call . . . Yes, yes, Frida was very sick, but that was nothing new or unexpected.

Even through the fog of her fever, she heard the urgency in the doctor's grave voice. And she heard the Maestro's tired, irritable response. Something inside her finally snapped. The imaginary cracked column collapsed, her spine broke in two and the thin thread that had been keeping her there snapped.

The time has come, she decided, the time has come.

The last time she had tried to kill herself it had been a rash, desperate and amateurish attempt at a moment when she was beside herself. She had taken her stash of pills from the drawer, shaken them out into the palm of her hand and swallowed them. The last thing she remembered was that her eyelids and limbs felt as heavy as lead. She had not prepared herself, it had simply been an act of desperation.

At least she had been able to see how easy it was to leave this world, she thought. This time, though, she was making a rational, mature decision, while she was still in full control. She wanted to be in control until the end. She was too familiar with death to be willing to go on its terms. She herself would determine the conditions of her death, as she had of her life. She knew that many would think how somebody who loved life so much would never raise a hand against herself, but they didn't realize that this was exactly the point: if you take your own life you do it to trump death by choosing the moment yourself.

Later, when her doctor and visitors had left and she and the Maestro were alone, she took out a beautiful antique gold ring. Why are you giving this to me now? the Maestro asked in surprise.

Because I have a feeling I'll be leaving you soon, she replied.

But he was not listening, he did not hear her words. As so many times before, she had the feeling that words were oozing out of her mouth like spittle, while to him they were just disjointed noises, a torrent of nonsensical ramblings. Maybe he didn't hear her because he saw her opening her mouth like a fish with no sound coming out. Or maybe the meaning of her words escaped him, their sound bouncing off him like an empty echo. You're not hearing me, you're not hearing me, she would scream, beating his chest with her fists to his shocked surprise. But she had no energy left for further explanation.

She was sure the Maestro would fix it so that her suicide did not cause a scandal. He had done it before for that girl. Nobody ever heard a peep about what had happened. He would do it for himself as much as for her. The Maestro would not let suicide spoil the image of his wife as a fantastic woman, the radiant, strong and cheerful Frida, who lived and painted despite all her travails. Nobody cared about the frail, desperate Frida who could not paint anymore, the Frida whose body was being eroded by infection and whose spirit was being eroded by drugs.

The doctors, of course, would find some probable cause of death and that would be the official version. The image of Frida and her invincible spirit would be preserved for posterity.

Only her diary, paintings and drawings of those last few months testified to her disintegration and to her awareness of it.

But Frida knew that her myth was already stronger than the truth and that nobody would believe in her suicide anyway.

Where are you now, Kity?

Soon, you will walk into the room and find my body in bed, turning cold. The first thing you will do, I know, is touch my face in disbelief, because, strangely enough, death always comes unexpectedly, even when it is a matter of mere days or hours. So I hope you will compose yourself quickly and close my mouth. You just have to snap shut my jaw before rigor mortis sets in. I don't know if it is because that is where the deceased's soul flies out, but I would certainly agree that the sight of a mouth gaping open is pretty disgusting.

Then you will kiss me and your tears will spill onto my face and onto my hair, which will keep growing. I remember how we used to read about it in bed when we were children, how we couldn't believe that a person's hair and nails keep growing for days after they die. What's death, you asked me, when is somebody actually dead? Now I can tell you: biological functions don't matter. What matters is meaning. Death is when you've got nothing of *your own* life left anymore, and you don't care whether you are still breathing or your hair and nails are still growing. You yourself don't exist anymore. So dry your tears, Kity. I'm at peace about leaving because this is no longer me; just look at my last paintings and you will understand. Anyway, caring for me has become too much of a burden and pointless. I'm simply accelerating my departure a little, that's all, just enough so that it is I, not death, who decides when my time has come.

I don't know if I would have lasted this long without you . . . if you hadn't watched over me and made sure that I ate that revolting soup and mush, that I took my pills on time and went to sleep. You washed and dressed me, gave me my injections, wrapped my miserable stump. You slept in the house and kept me company when the Maestro lost the energy and will to do it himself. I can't tell you how hurt I was when I saw you in bed with the Maestro. When I painted that butchered woman with all that blood gushing out I never told you that in my mind the killer was not the Maestro, it was you.

Yes, I was like a corpse after that, drained of life. Love breaks you; first you are whole and then you are smashed to pieces, like a walnut. You see your wounds, your bare, bleeding insides. I believed in his love because it was the answer to all my questions, the solution to my suffering. In my mind, his love had the power to cure my sickness, to rescue me from loneliness. I believed that love could resurrect the dead. It was hard for me to bear your betrayal and his. Especially yours. But it shattered all my illusions, at least. I realized that I had been relying on this love like a crutch, like my corset, to help me survive.

All the same, I couldn't give you or the Maestro up. My fear of languishing in solitude was greater than my anger or the contempt I felt for the two of you. Later your tender devotion helped to heal the wound you inflicted on me. You, of course, knew much more about "love" than I did, about how brutal it can be. Your husband beat you, you were left on your own with two children, you could have few illusions about love, men, marriage. But I was blind and insatiable. I was scared, Kity, of being left to myself and my sickness. Forgive me my selfishness if you can.

Later I was grateful; it was because of you that I turned seriously to painting. When the pain became unbearable, when it threatened to engulf me, I had to get it out of my system.

The sicker I was, the more remote the Maestro became. Nobody but you could have endured so much. Sickness doesn't bring people closer together, it drives them apart—first comes the pity, then the physical separation. And who wouldn't have run away, if only from the stench of my body? There was a time when he would lie down beside me and read or talk to me until I fell asleep. Toward the end, I had to beg him to at least sit next to me, if only for a bit. Even that was too much for him. He was always in a hurry, always had to leave. I stopped asking where he was going.

When I was incarcerated in that plaster corset and my back had turned into a pile of pus, it was you who dressed the repulsive wounds on my back. It was you who wiped my ass clean when I couldn't go to the toilet. Like a penitent, and maybe that's what you were. Maybe that was the punishment you had meted out to yourself, maybe this penitence was your way of atonement. You could have let others do it, the nurses or the maid. But you didn't. How you wept when you washed my leg before it was amputated. You were so gentle, so careful, as if washing your own child, not my withered, gangrenous leg. And in honesty, sometimes I *was* your child, demanding and spoiled, not at all like your own two angels.

If I add it all up, here's what I get: thirty-two operations in my forty-seven years of life. When you think that I had my first operation at the age of eighteen, then it works out to more than one operation a year. My only consolation, if consolation it is, is that I made as much out of my life as I could.

My darling baby sister, this body of mine has always been my prison. Now it is becoming my grave.

The loneliness was always worse than the pain, she thought; pain had condemned her to a lifetime of loneliness.

Now there was no Kity. There was no ether. The syringe was her instrument of death. Without hesitation she reached out and picked it up. It was cold to the touch. Calmly, she filled it with the fluid from the little bottles that she had warmed in her hand. She thought how the dark cloud from her childhood had finally caught up with her. Its heavy shadow loomed over her once more, but she had nowhere to run. Nor did she want to run. She was without expectations, without hope. But at least she had the strength to stay true to herself.

Was that the familiar stench of pity she smelled in the roses that Kity had brought? It's all right for the living to pity the dying, she thought, because they are really only pitying themselves.

For a moment she felt light, as if she were flying and could see everything from above. At last she felt the way she had always wanted to feel: like a butterfly. She imagined the house after she was gone, her room, her empty bed. She knew that the Maestro, Kity, her friends would all be sad, for a while. They would think of her, for a while. And then later, occasionally. She would become a distant memory. She was already a memory and glad of it. She was no longer the Frida they knew because what she was now was not her.

Only her paintings were her.

Her final thought was that this taking of her own life, this last act of her own free will, this tiny prick of the needle, was actually her last real defeat. Not the decision or act itself, but the manner of her leaving. The fact that, after all her efforts to survive, she was forced to take her own life with her very last ounce of strength.

Suddenly she remembered that before her last encounter with death, almost thirty years earlier, she had licked her lips with the taste of an orange. She had been alive, so unforgettably alive.

She did not even feel the prick of the needle. There was a blaze of white light.

White, not black, was the color of her death.

She thought she saw the door open and her nameless little childhood friend walk into the room. As once long ago, the little girl took her by the hand. And Frida surrendered to her touch.

They Would Never Hurt a Fly
War Criminals on Trial in The Hague
"Who were they? Ordinary people like you or me—or monsters?"
This is the question Slavenka Drakulić asks as she sets out to understand the people behind the horrific crimes committed during the war that ripped Yugoslavia apart in the 1990s. Drawing on first-hand observations of the trials, as well as other sources, Drakulić portrays some of the individuals accused of war crimes during one of the most brutal conflicts in Europe in the twentieth century, including former Serbian president Slobodan Miloševic; Radislav Krstic, the first to be sentenced for genocide; Biljana Plavšic, the only woman accused of war crimes; and Ratko Mladic, now in hiding.   *ISBN 978-0-14-303542-8*

S.
A Novel about the Balkans
Set in 1992, during the height of the war in Bosnia, *S.* is the story of a Bosnian woman in exile who has just given birth to an unwanted child—one without a country, a name, a father, or a language. Through a series of flashbacks, *S.* relives the unspeakable crimes she has endured, and in telling her story depicts the darkest side of human nature during wartime.   *ISBN 978-0-14-029844-4*

Café Europa
Life After Communism
Today in Eastern Europe the architectural work of revolution is complete. The old order has been replaced by various forms of free market economy and de jure democracy. But as Slavenka Drakulić observes, "in everyday life, the revolution consists much more of the small things—of sounds, looks and images." In this brilliant work of political reportage, we see that Europe remains a divided continent. In place of the fallen Berlin Wall there is a chasm between East and West, consisting of the different way people continue to live and understand the world. While intimations of the West are gradually making their way east—boutiques carrying Levis and tiny food shops called "Supermarket" multiplying on main boulevards—the acceptance of the East by the rest of Europe continues to prove much more elusive.   *ISBN 978-0-14-027772-2*